"Baby, you had an itch that needed scratching."

Paige's face turned white at Quinn's words.

He added, "Was it me who excited you, Paige? Or was it the idea of being taken by a stranger that turned you on?"

Tears rose to her eyes. "Quinn, please, it wasn't like that..."

He stared at her. "No wonder Alan fell for your act," he muttered.

Paige shook her head. "I never pretended with Alan. I told him I didn't love him."

"And what a nice touch that was," he said with a bitter laugh. "He practically blushed when he told me he was going to teach you about love."

Paige was filled with despair as Quinn looked at her with hate in his eyes.

"I'll bet you could write a book about *love*," he snarled.

SANDRA MARTON says she's always believed in romance. She wrote her first love story when she was nine and fell madly in love at sixteen with the man who is her husband. Today they live on Long Island, midway between the glitter of Manhattan and the quiet beaches of the Atlantic. Sandra is delighted to be writing the kinds of stories she loves and even happier to find that her readers enjoy them, too.

Books by Sandra Marton

HARLEQUIN PRESENTS

988—A GAME OF DECEIT
1027—OUT OF THE SHADOWS
1067—INTIMATE STRANGERS
1082—LOVESCENES
1121—HEART OF THE HAWK
1155—A FLOOD OF SWEET FIRE
1194—DEAL WITH THE DEVIL

Don't miss any of our special offers. Write to us at the following address for information on our newest releases.

Harlequin Reader Service
901 Fuhrmann Blvd., P.O. Box 1397, Buffalo, NY 14240
Canadian address: P.O. Box 603,
Fort Erie, Ont. L2A 5X3

SANDRA MARTON

cherish the flame

Harlequin Books

TORONTO • NEW YORK • LONDON
AMSTERDAM • PARIS • SYDNEY • HAMBURG
STOCKHOLM • ATHENS • TOKYO • MILAN

For Elizabeth,
who made all this possible.

Harlequin Presents first edition November 1989
ISBN 0-373-11219-X

Original hardcover edition published in 1988
by Mills & Boon Limited

CHAPTER ONE

THE ALL HALLOWS EVE MASQUERADE BALL was in full swing the first time Paige Gardiner saw him. He was leaning against the far wall of the Hunt Club ballroom, watching the gyrating devils and black cats on the crowded dance-floor. There was a dangerous look about him, a leanly muscled power that was disturbing, and Paige thought suddenly of a lion in the tall grass, waiting for a herd of wildebeest to move just a bit closer.

'Paige, for heaven's sake, haven't you spotted Alan yet? We can't just stand here, blocking the doorway all evening.'

Paige blinked and looked at her mother. 'Sorry,' she said, giving her a quick smile. 'I'm trying to find him, Mother. I just can't seem to . . .'

'Of course you can't. There must be a dozen Romeos here tonight.' Her mother sighed and brushed a lock of Paige's pale blonde hair back from her face. 'And a dozen Juliets, of course. But none as beautiful as you, dear.'

Paige smiled. 'And no Romeos as handsome as my fiancé,' she said. 'That's why he'll be easy to find.'

But he wasn't. She frowned behind the anonymity of her delicate silver mask as her violet eyes searched the crowded room. There was, indeed, an over-abundance of Romeos, and from this distance they all looked very much alike. Still, Alan was special. He was the man she was engaged to marry. She'd be able to pick him out from all the rest.

There he was again, the man she'd seen when she entered the ballroom. He was looking through the glass doors at the club's formal gardens. His back was to her now, but Paige knew it was he. She recognised the defiant set of his shoulders beneath his dinner-jacket, and the too-proud angle of his head.

He turned suddenly, and his eyes, behind his narrow black mask, locked with hers. The ballroom, the dancers, the music—all of it spun away.

'Paige?' Her father's hand closed around her arm. 'Paige, isn't that Alan?'

An eternity seemed to pass before she could look away from the man and turn towards her father.

'Where?' she asked, and he nodded towards a nearby Romeo. 'I . . . I'm not certain,' she said, and colour rushed into her cheeks. Ridiculous, she thought. She'd been dating Alan Fowler for almost a year and she'd been engaged to him for three weeks. Surely she could recognise him, even in costume. 'Alan?' she said tentatively. 'Is that you?' To Paige's great relief, the Romeo turned and smiled.

'There you are, sweetheart.' She smiled in return as he took her hands in his and kissed her cheek. 'You look positively beautiful, Juliet.'

'You look pretty good yourself, Romeo,' she said, and she smiled again. 'Is it my imagination, or is every pair of eyes in the room on us?'

Alan grinned as he tucked her hand into the crook of his arm. 'It's a possibility,' he said. 'Mother's out-of-town guests have been arriving by the carload all day long. In fact, Aunt Dorothy was asking about you only a few minutes ago. Want to meet her?'

'Not yet,' Paige said so quickly that everyone laughed.

'Paige is nervous about meeting all your relatives,' Paige's mother said as she brushed an imaginary speck of lint from her daughter's gown.

'It just doesn't seem like the best way to do it, that's all,' Paige murmured. 'You know, at a costume ball, with so much going on all at once.'

Janet Gardiner sighed. 'There's not much choice, with the wedding only three days off.'

Alan laughed. 'Mother thinks it's terrific. She must have rented a dozen costumes and . . .' He looked down at Paige as she shuddered lightly. 'Are you cold, sweetheart? Here,' he said, slipping his arm around her shoulders, 'is that better?'

Paige nodded. 'Much,' she said brightly. 'I just felt a chill, that's all.'

Three days, she thought, as Alan turned towards her father and began to discuss a business matter. Three days, and she would be Mrs Alan Fowler. It seemed impossible. A month ago she'd been content, dating Alan as she had been for months, turning aside his proposals which had become so frequent she hardly noticed them. But then, there had been that one evening when he put his finger to her lips before she could refuse him.

'Don't say no this time, Paige,' he'd pleaded. 'How about something different? Tell me you'll think it over until tomorrow.'

'I won't be here tomorrow,' she'd said. 'Remember? Maywalk's is sending me on my first buying trip this week. I won't be back until Friday.'

Alan had grinned. 'Even better. I'll have a whole week to hope—and you'll have a whole week to think of a reason not to say "yes".'

And Paige had smiled and agreed. After all, she owed him that much. Alan was sweet and charming, and she knew that the women he'd dated before would give anything to change places with her. Their dates always ended with chaste goodnight kisses, but that didn't seem to deter him. If anything, her refusals to make their relationship more intimate seemed only to spur him into a more determined pursuit. What harm could there be in letting five days go by before telling him 'no' one more time?

But, when she'd returned that Friday, her mother had embraced her and said tearfully, 'I'm so happy for you, dear. But you should have told us yourself.' And while Paige was still trying to make sense out of that, her father had kissed her and told her he was glad she'd finally decided to take his advice and marry Alan.

'I've been telling you he's the right man for months,' he'd said. 'I'm glad you finally came to your senses, girl.'

And Alan—Alan had flashed his sheepish, charming grin and admitted he'd got carried away, that he'd mentioned what she'd said, but only to her parents and his, and . . .

'What do you mean, you mentioned what I'd said?' Paige had demanded angrily. 'I didn't say anything, Alan. You asked me to wait, to think things over . . .'

Alan had said yes, he knew that, but what was there to think about, really? They liked each other, they had fun together, and he would give her a secure, happy life.

'Don't be angry with me, sweetheart,' he'd murmured.

His expression had been so apologetic that Paige's anger had fallen away. 'I'm not angry. It's just that . . .' She'd touched her hand gently to his cheek. 'You must know that I don't love you, Alan. Well, I mean, I love you, but I'm not in love with you. Do you understand? You deserve more from a wife than I can give you.'

Alan knew what she meant. He'd taken her in his arms a dozen times, waiting patiently for her to respond to his caresses, assuring her it was all right when she didn't.

'I want you,' he'd said simply, smiling into her eyes. 'As for the rest—it will come in time. You'll see.'

Embarrassment coloured her cheeks, but her gaze had never wavered. 'Alan, what if I don't? What if . . .'

The look on his face had told her he couldn't imagine such a thing happening.

'I'd still love you, of course,' he'd said, and then he'd grinned boyishly. 'But there's no danger of that. I won't fail you, Paige. You'll see.'

'Alan,' Paige had said, wanting to tell him it wasn't his failure she was concerned about, but he'd taken her in his arms and kissed her again, and when finally she'd pushed him gently from her the door had swung open and his mother had entered the room.

'Paige, we're so pleased,' she'd said. 'I hope you don't mind—I've spoken to the caterer—I thought perhaps we'd have a champagne breakfast, with quail and lobster.'

And after that, Paige thought as Alan led her to the dance-floor, after that, everything had moved far too quickly. Alan's father wanted him to head up the South American branch of the firm, which meant that the wedding that had been planned for next June was moved back to November, and the long engagement Paige had anticipated had become one of the shortest on record. *Three days*, she thought again, as his arms slipped around her, *three days . . .*

'Hey,' Alan said gently, 'come back, Paige.'

Paige looked up at him and shook her head. 'Sorry. I was just thinking—I can't believe the wedding day's so soon.'

He drew back and grinned down at her. 'It's too late to get out of it. What would Aunt Dorothy think?'

Paige gave him a quick smile. 'That I was silly to give you up.'

Alan laughed as he spun her across the dance-floor. 'That she'd been done out of the chance to attend the party of the year. Aunt Dorothy and Mother spent half the morning talking about Mother's plans for the wedding.'

'Only half the morning? I'd think our wedding deserved more than that.'

'It did. Aunt Dorothy spent the rest of the time giving me the benefit of her experience.'

Paige laughed. 'Is she an expert?'

'In a way.' He grinned and drew her closer. 'The old

girl's been married three times. I'll probably have to listen to more advice from my big brother, too.'

She laughed again. 'Don't tell me he's been married three times.'

Alan chuckled. 'Quinn? Not likely. No woman's ever going to catch him.'

'Terrific,' Paige said teasingly. 'What kind of advice can you get from someone like that?'

'A speech that starts, "You've got to be crazy to do this, old man". You know, the usual "I'm older and wiser" nonsense big brothers always give.'

'And when do I get to meet this paragon?' Paige asked, tilting her head to the side and smiling at her fiancé.

'As soon as he gets here. He's due tomorrow, but with Quinn you never know. He . . .'

'Alan, you don't mind if I dance with my daughter, do you?'

Paige looked up as Alan let go of her and her father took her into his arms.

'Of course not, sir. Paige, sweetheart, I'll get us some champagne, OK? I'll be back in a minute.'

Her father cleared his throat as Paige settled into his arms. 'Your mother's worried about you,' he said without any preliminaries. 'She sent me to ask if everything was all right.'

Paige looked at Andrew Gardiner in surprise. 'What do you mean, Father?'

'She says you've been acting as if you were a million miles away.' The music changed to an old-fashioned waltz and her father guided her across the floor. 'I told her it was just last-minute jitters.'

Paige nodded. 'I guess.'

Her father peered into her face. 'Alan is right for you, Paige. He's a fine young man. I've got to know him during the years I've worked for his father, and . . .'

It was the same speech her father had been making for months, ever since she had let slip the fact that Alan had proposed.

'Father,' she said gently, 'you can relax. I'm marrying him, remember? I finally took your advice.'

Her father looked at her. 'I only want what's best for all of us.'

Paige laughed. 'All of us? I'm the one who's getting married, not you.'

'It's just a figure of speech, child. You know what I mean—if you're happy, your mother and I are happy.' Her father smiled at her. 'You are happy, aren't you?'

Paige nodded. Of course she was. Alan was, as her father had insisted, a fine man, and she did love him—in a way. And, if that was enough for him, it was enough for her. It was more than enough for her, she told herself as her father waltzed her around the dance-floor. She'd had her taste of what everyone called the great passion, and she knew it for the fiction it was. She'd tried to tell that to Alan the day they'd become engaged, but he hadn't given her the chance. And it was just as well. Perhaps he could teach her heart to soar and her pulse to sing. And if he couldn't, then his pleasure would give her pleasure. That would be enough. It might even be best. It would . . .

A chill danced across her shoulders. Someone was watching her; she knew it without question, just as she knew who it was. The strange man she'd noticed an enternity ago—it had to be him. She could sense his presence, feel his power.

Paige drew closer into her father's arms. He smiled at her and she smiled back, but her eyes swept the room. Her breath caught in her throat. Yes, yes, there he was, standing on the perimeter of the dance-floor, his jacket open, revealing a taut expanse of white silk shirt that clung to his chest as if it were a second skin. His hands were tucked into his trouser pockets and the material strained across his thighs. He was balanced on legs slightly apart, and his head was cocked to the side—and he was watching her. Behind the black mask, his eyes were fixed on her, burning into her, stripping her of the long, silk gown, moving now to the full curve of her breasts, watching their all too rapid rise and fall above the low-cut neckline.

Paige stumbled and her father's arms tightened around her.

'Paige? What's wrong?'

'Nothing,' she said quickly. 'Nothing,' she repeated, tearing her eyes from the man and looking at her father. 'I just—I must be tired.'

Her father nodded. 'It's been a busy week for you.' He looked into her eyes and frowned. 'Would you like to sit down?'

He'll come to you if you do. You know he will . . .

A tremor went through her. 'No,' she said quickly. 'I . . . I want to dance with you, Father. Really. I . . .' She swallowed and then ran her tongue across her dry lips. 'That man,' she said, her voice a breathy whisper, 'I wondered—do you know who he is?'

'Which man?'

'That one, over there,' she said urgently, taking a few steps so that her father had to turn around and look in the direction she'd been facing. 'The tall one, beside the dance-floor.'

'Which man?' her father repeated. 'What kind of costume is he wearing?'

'He's not in costume,' Paige said, looking over her shoulder. 'He . . .'

He was gone. Her eyes scanned the crowd, searching for him, but he had disappeared. Her heart was racing as if she'd been running instead of dancing, and it seemed suddenly hard to breath.

Andrew Gardiner grasped his daughter by the shoulders and held her steady.

'What is it? Do you feel ill?'

I don't know how I feel. Excited. Exhilarated. Terrified ...

Paige drew a deep breath. 'I ... I think it's time I went to the ladies' room and checked my make-up,' she said. She smiled, and the wary expression on her father's face told her the smile looked as artificial as it felt. 'After all, I want to look my best for all Alan's relatives.'

'Let me get your mother. She'll go with you.'

'No,' she said again, more sharply this time. 'There's no reason to bother Mother.' Paige patted her father's arm. 'I'll just be a few minutes, Father. Really. If Alan comes looking for me, tell him I'll be right back.'

'Paige ...'

Her father's voice drifted after her as she hurried across the dance-floor. This was the price you paid for too little sleep and too much to do, she thought as she wound her way through the crowded ballroom. She was lightheaded, and who wouldn't be after the day she'd had? Up at dawn, so that her mother could make some last-minute adjustments to her dress and veil. And then there'd been lunch with the girls she'd worked with, and tea with her bridesmaids ...

'Excuse me,' Paige said as she moved between a laughing Marie Antoinette and a smiling Satan. Alan would understand if she begged off and asked him to take her home. She'd meet his relatives first, his Aunt Dorothy and all the rest, and then go home and get out of her costume and into a warm bath. The ballroom was just too crowded, the music too loud, the air too thick and warm. She'd comb her hair, touch up her make-up, go off and say all the right things to Alan's family and that would be that. In three days, she could relax. In three days, all this would be over. Three days. Oh, God, three days ...

There was a long queue in the ladies' room. 'I only want to get to the sink,' Paige said, but it was impossible to move past anyone in the narrow space. She took a deep breath and settled in to wait her return behind a harem girl and a lady pirate.

'. . . just popped the question,' the harem girl bubbled, holding out her left hand. 'Look, isn't it lovely?'

The lady pirate and everyone else looked at the girl's ring finger and smiled. A diamond gleamed on it, a diamond considerably smaller than the one on Paige's hand. But Paige knew, without question, that her eyes had never gleamed with the radiance she saw reflected in the harem girl's eyes. Suddenly, she wondered if the girl's heart raced when her fiancé looked at her, whether she ever found it difficult to breathe after his eyes had met hers and discovered secrets she'd never acknowledged. Paige had never felt that way under Alan's gaze. She'd never felt that way in her life, not even during that one, long-ago love-affair, never felt that way until moments ago when a man whose name she didn't know had looked at her from behind a black mask.

The harem girl fell silent as a strangled gasp came from Paige's throat.

'Excuse me,' she said, and she tried to smile. But she couldn't; she could feel her lips draw back from her teeth in a terrible parody of a smile as she turned and shouldered her way past the waiting women. 'Excuse me,' she said again, ignoring the raised eyebrows and curious faces that turned in her direction.

Finally, back in the ballroom, Paige leaned back against the door to the ladies' room and looked around her. *Alan*, she thought, willing him to appear before her. But, if Alan Fowler was one of the Romeos nearby, it was impossible for her to pick him out.

The music seemed louder than ever, the crowd denser. A

heavy-set man in a pirate costume was smoking a cigar. The smell of it seemed to engulf her. Paige thought of pushing her way out of the ballroom to the street. She could flag a taxi and go home . . .

But there was no street outside the Hunt Club, there was only a car park high on a Connecticut bluff overlooking the Atlantic. And she couldn't just disappear into the night. Alan and her parents would worry, they'd come looking for her. And what would she tell them when they found her? Could she say, I saw a girl in the ladies' room, and she was so happy about her engagement that it made me want to cry? Could she say, I saw a man I've never seen before, a man whose name I don't know, and he made me feel something Alan never made me feel, and it frightened me so much that I ran away?

The room seemed to quiver around her. 'Dear God,' she whispered aloud, and suddenly an arm slid around her waist. She smelled a faint tang of leathery cologne, felt the brush of fabric against her cheek, felt the hard length of a male body against hers.

'You'll be all right,' a deep voice said. 'Just lean on me.'

'I . . . I'm fine,' she said. 'Really . . .'

But she allowed herself to lean into the man's embrace. His arm tightened around her, his hand pressing against the curve of her hip.

'You're going to pass out if you don't get some fresh air,' he said. 'Take a deep breath. That's it.'

Paige did as she was told. She'd never fainted in her life, but she thought he was probably right. The room was a spinning vortex of bright colours, the music a drumming shriek. She fitted her body to his, almost burrowing against him as he led her through the crowd. The doors that led to the gardens loomed ahead, and she knew that was where he was taking her.

He reached for the door and pushed it open. A gust of

cold air blew into her face, clearing the cobwebs from her mind. It was time for her to stop him. She could thank him for his help and asked him to locate her fiancé for her.

But she would do none of that. Paige knew it, even before he led her into the chill October garden, just as she knew that the man beside her was the stranger who'd been watching her all evening, and the race of her heart only confirmed what she could no longer deny.

She had wanted this moment to come. She had been hoping it would. And now that it was here, she knew her life would never be the same again.

CHAPTER TWO

PAIGE shivered as the glass doors swung shut behind her. The last time she'd been here was with Alan. Roses and honeysuckle had perfumed the air then. Now it smelled of the sea that beat relentlessly at the sand below the bluff. Music spilled faintly from the closed ballroom, a soft accompaniment to the distant pound of the surf. A full moon lit the terrace, but as Paige lifted her eyes to the stranger's face a bank of clouds scudded across the sky, plunging everything into darkness.

Every instinct told her to pull free of the arm encircling her waist and hurry back into lighted warmth of the clubhouse, but her feet seemed rooted to the ground. This is insanity, she thought, and she turned to say she was leaving. But the man beside her spoke first.

'Take a deep breath.'

Paige shook her head. 'I'm all right now. I . . .'

She felt the pressure of his hand. 'Do it,' he said curtly. 'Go on. Inhale.'

It was a command, not a suggestion. She nodded and did as he'd said, drawing the cool air deep into her lungs.

'Better?'

She nodded again. 'Yes. Much better. Thank you for your . . .'

'Don't talk,' he said. 'Just take another breath.'

She inhaled again and told herself there was nothing to be concerned about. She was sure she'd turned as pale as a sheet in that stuffy ballroom. He'd noticed, and he'd come to her assistance. He was just being a Good Samaritan.

Anything else was the result of an over-active imagination.

'I . . . I'm fine now,' she said. 'And I'm terribly sorry for all the trouble I've caused you.'

'It was no trouble at all.' The pressure of his hand urged her to turn towards him. 'In fact, you might say you did me a favour.'

'I did?' Was there a smile in his voice? If only she could see his face . . .

He laughed softly. 'I've always wanted to rescue a damsel in distress, Juliet.' His hand touched her cheek. 'That is your name tonight, isn't it?'

'I . . . yes, yes, that's right,' Paige said quickly. 'And I really have to go inside now. My fiancé . . .'

His fingers closed on her hand. 'I thought I saw something sparkling on your finger. Tell me, Juliet—where is he? Your fiancé, I mean.'

'He . . . he's in the ballroom, waiting for me. He . . . What are you doing?' she asked, even though the answer was obvious. He had shrugged free of his dinner-jacket and was draping it over her shoulders.

'You're cold,' he said, lifting the curtain of pale hair from her shoulders and settling it over the jacket. 'Your hand's like ice.'

'I'm not,' she said quickly. 'I'm fine. I . . .'

'Don't argue with me,' he said as he drew the lapels together.

No one argued with this man, Paige thought suddenly. No one would dare. His fingers brushed against her skin, his thumbs skimming her throat, lingering against the hollows above her collarbone. She wondered if he could feel the quick leap of blood that pulsed beneath his touch, and a tremor went through her.

'Maybe I am a little chilly,' she said, and she gave a forced laugh. 'It's cold out here, isn't it? It's the ocean, I guess. Although, of course, it's autumn . . .'

Damn! She was babbling like a fool. She sounded, she thought, like a nervous schoolgirl. And that was exactly how she felt—like a teenager at her first dance, alone with a boy she had a crush on. But it was a man beside her in the darkness, not a boy, a man whose name she didn't know. *What are you doing here, Paige?*

'Walk with me,' he said, clasping her hand in his.

'I can't,' she said, but he was already leading her along the path that bordered the garden. 'Please . . .'

'Just for a few minutes.'

She felt as if she were caught in a dream, her only link to reality the faint music drifting from the lighted ballroom. The man beside her was tall, taller than she'd thought. Even in high-heeled sandals, Paige reached only to his shoulder. His jacket hung about her like a cloak, the shoulders and sleeves trailing as if she were a child playing at dressing up. He'd raised the collar when he slipped it around her, and the soft wool brushed against her cheek. It felt warm to the touch, as if it still carried the heat of his body. And she could smell his scent on the fabric, that same cologne she'd noticed earlier, mixed with something much more basic and sensual. It was a clean, masculine odour that was his alone.

For one swift beat of her heart, Paige closed her eyes and breathed it in, letting the smell and the heat of him surround her. Then, with a rush, her lashes flew open. What was she doing? Here she was, traipsing along in the dark beside a man she didn't know, heart racing, throat dry, never once thinking of Alan or the engagement ring on her finger or the wedding vows she'd take in three days' time . . .

His hand clasped hers more tightly. 'Don't be afraid,' he said softly.

She managed another forced laugh. 'I'm not,' she said. 'I . . .'

'You are. I can feel your pulse racing.' He stopped and turned towards her, his fingers skimming the tender skin on the inside of her wrist. 'Your heart's beating like a frightened rabbit's.'

Paige took a hurried step back. 'I . . . I have to go back now,' she said in a whisper. 'Thanks for your jacket. Let me . . .'

His hand tightened on her wrist. 'Don't go,' he said. His voice was low and husky.

Her tongue felt thick in her mouth. 'I must,' she said quickly. 'My fiancé . . .'

The man shook his head in a gesture of impatience. 'The hell with your fiancé,' he said roughly. 'Stay here, with me.'

His hands cupped her face, tilting it up to him. There was a ring on his finger, an old one, set with a ruby. The blood-red stone captured the pale moonlight and warmed it with a sprakling fire.

She felt the warmth of his breath against her skin. His features were in shadow but Paige knew them, just as she knew that she had known this man since the beginning of for ever, that she had belonged to him in another time, in another eternity. His head bent to hers, and she closed her eyes, waiting, waiting . . .

There was a sound in the silent darkness. The wind sighing through the trees or a wave building against the shore below—she wasn't sure—but it was enough to bring her to her senses.

'I must go back,' she said, and she pulled away from him. 'I'm grateful for your help. I . . . I don't know what happened to me in there . . .'

The brave words died as he moved towards her. 'You know what happened,' he said.

There was something in his voice, a sense of certainty, that both thrilled and terrified her. She knew that he wasn't referring to her sudden dizziness. He meant that hushed moment of eternity they had shared—and she wasn't going to talk about that. Not now, not ever—and certainly not with him.

'You're right,' she said quickly, 'I do know. I felt sick, that's all. It was warm in the ballroom. And crowded. And . . .'

She gasped as his hands slid to her shoulders and bit into her flesh. 'Don't lie to me, Juliet.'

'I'm not lying. I . . .'

'I've been watching you all evening.'

Her skin tingled beneath the heat of his fingers. 'What are you talking about?'

He laughed softly. 'Are we going to play games? You know I've been watching you.'

She felt a sudden rush of heat flood her cheeks. Thank God for the darkness, she thought.

'You're wrong,' she said. 'I . . .'

His hands clasped her more tightly. 'You were watching me, too,' he said, slowly drawing her towards him.

Paige's denial was swift. 'I wasn't. I never noticed you at all until you offered to help me.'

'Who were you loking for when you came into the ballroom, Juliet?' She saw the white flash of his teeth. 'Your fiancé?'

'Yes, my fiancé,' she said quickly, grasping the word as if it would save her from whatever might come next, 'that's right. And he's probably looking for me right now. He . . .'

'Hell, he should have been with you all evening.' His hands moved over her shoulders. 'I'd have been, if you belonged to me.'

'I don't belong to anyone. And he *was* waiting. I mean, I just didn't see him right away. I . . .'

He laughed softly. 'But you saw me.' His hands slid from her shoulders, down her arms, and encircled her wrists. 'And then the crowd closed in and I lost sight of you. Is that when your Romeo found you?'

Paige's lips felt parched. Carefully, she ran the tip of her tongue over them.

'Yes. And now I really have to go back to him. I . . .'

'The next time I saw you, you were dancing with an older man.' He lifted her hands between them and held them against his chest. 'It wasn't Romeo.'

It was a statement, not a question. Despite herself, Paige smiled. 'No.'

He nodded. 'Your father, I thought. Or a favourite uncle.'

'My father,' she said. 'I saw you watching us. I . . .'

The admission was out before she had time to stop it. Any hope Paige had that it might slip by vanished when she heard the stranger's softly triumphant laugh.

'But you said you hadn't noticed me at all, Juliet.'

'That's not my name,' she said desperately. 'That's fantasy . . .'

His arms slid around her. 'This is a night of fantasy,' he whispered. 'Anything can happen on a night like this.' Slowly, he drew her closer to him. 'You can even stay here and dance with me.'

The music drifting from the ballroom had turned slow and dreamlike. Paige put her hands on his chest as he began to move to its faint rhythm.

'Don't, please . . .' She stood stiffly within his arms, fighting against the desire to melt against him, and then she drew in her breath. A night of fantasy, he'd said, and that was what this was, wasn't it? Harmless fantasy. The stuff of dreams. Her heart turned over. 'All right,' she whispered. 'Just one dance . . .'

'One dance,' he said easily. 'And then we'll do whatever you want.'

We'll do whatever you want . . . Was there a threat in the simple words? No, not a threat, Paige told herself as they began to move across the flagstones. His words held something more. An assurance, a conviction that he knew what she wanted, even if she hadn't admitted it to herself yet.

The stranger could think what he liked. One dance with him—that was all—and then she'd return to Alan's side. And she'd tell Alan about all this in a week or two, tell him about the bit of foolishness that had taken hold of her on this night three days before their wedding. They would laugh about it, just as they'd laughed about the bachelor party Alan's groomsmen had planned for tomorrow evening at a club known for its scantily clad barmaids.

'A rite of passage,' Alan called it, and that was what tonight was, wasn't it? This dance with a stranger was just one last taste of freedom, and Alan would smile when she told him about it and . . .

Who was she kidding? She could never tell Alan. She could never tell anyone. This was insanity. Dangerous insanity. It wasn't a last fling or an innocent rite of passage . . .

The man drew her closer. 'Are your eyes really the colour of spring violets?'

His voice, soft and husky, moved over her like a velvet caress. In the heavy silence of the night, Paige could hear the quick tumble of her heart.

'Who are you?' she asked breathlessly.

He laughed softly. 'You know who I am, Juliet. I'm the man who's wanted to make love to you all night.'

The admission stole her breath away. She stumbled and he caught her to him, holding her tightly against the hardness of his body.

'Don't,' she whispered, but, even as she said the word, she felt herself melting against him. Her hands spread against his chest; she felt the thudding beat of his heart beneath her palms.

'Juliet . . .'

A door slammed behind them. There was a sudden shriek of laughter, and the sound of feet on the gravel path. Paige's return to reality was swift. Her hands balled into fists and pressed against him.

'Let me go,' she said in a desperate whisper. 'Please . . .'

His hand caught hers. 'Come with me,' he said in a low voice.

'Are you crazy? My fiancé . . .'

'I don't give a damn about your fiancé. And neither do you. Hell, if he mattered, you wouldn't be here with me.'

His words sent a chill through her. 'You don't know what you're saying. He means everything to me. He . . .'

'Then you have nothing to fear by coming with me, do you?' His fingers wove through hers. 'Besides, if someone were to find us here, they might come to the wrong conclusion.'

She wanted to tell him that Alan would understand, but it was a hope, not a certainty. The footsteps and the laughter were growing closer. The man sensed her hesitancy and clasped her hand more tightly in his.

'We'll finish our dance,' he said as he drew her after him. 'Down there, on the beach. And then, if that's what you want, I'll return you to your Romeo.'

It was lunacy to follow him along the narrow gravel path that led down the bluff. Paige told herself that, even as she walked alongside him. It was lunacy to kick off her sandals and step into his waiting arms when her feet touched the sand. But it felt wonderful to let herself lean into his embrace and move in rhythm with the music. Moments passed, and she closed her eyes and put her head against his shoulder. When his lips brushed her hair, it seemed so right that she made no objection.

'Juliet,' he whispered.

Paige lifted her head slowly. The stranger's hand moved

up her back, to the nape of her neck, and his fingers twined in her hair.

'Juliet,' he said again, and, as the moon escaped the pursuing clouds and lit his face, her eyes filled with him, drinking in the features she had only glimpsed until now. His nose was narrow, his mouth hard, the bottom lip full and sensual. His eyes glittered behind the mask. Blue, she thought, while her heart drummed in her chest. Blue, or perhaps green . . .

As if he were reading her mind, he reached up and slowly pulled the black domino from his face. Her breathing quickened as he cast it aside and gazed at her. His eyes were a piercing aquamarine, the colour of the summer sea, deep-set and thickly lashed.

'Now it's your turn,' he murmured.

Paige trembled as he reached towards her. His fingers closed on the silver mask, and she held her breath as he untied it. Slowly, patiently, he eased it from her, and she knew she had never felt as naked in a man's arms as she felt at this moment. His eyes moving over her unmasked face were more intimate a caress than any she had ever experienced. God, what was happening to her?

'I knew your eyes were the colour of violets,' he said, smiling down at her. His voice thickened. 'You're beautiful, Juliet.'

His hand cupped her face. He was going to kiss her, she thought. She had to stop him . . .

Paige swayed as her lashes fell to her cheeks. What was the sense of pretending? She wanted him to kiss her. She knew it—and the stranger knew it. He'd been making love to her all night, first in the ballroom, then on the terrace, and now—now he was going to kiss her. The kiss would end the fantasy and bring back reality. It would put a stop to all this foolishness. She'd step back and apologise for letting things get out of hand and . . .

His mouth brushed against hers, the kiss as light as blown spray from the ocean.

'A flower,' he whispered as his arms curved around her. 'Your mouth is a flower that tastes of nectar as sweet as honey.' His head bent to hers and he kissed her again, the press of his mouth firmer, the kiss longer. When at last he lifted his head, Paige was breathless. 'So sweet,' he said, 'so wonderful . . .'

'Kiss me again,' she sighed.

His eyes changed, darkened to the colour of the ocean depths, and he gathered her to him. When his mouth dropped to hers, his lips were hungry and demanded surrender, and she gave it willingly. Her mouth softened beneath his, parted, and with a sound that was half-growl, half-triumph, he pulled her against him, moulding her body to his. Her fingers curled into the silky hair at the back of his head as his tongue touched her mouth with flame.

'I want to make love to you,' he whispered, drawing away only enough so he could look into her flushed face.

Some last link of reality made her shake her head.

'No,' she said, 'I can't . . .'

His hand slid to her breast, and she gasped as she felt the heat of his caress through the thin silk bodice.

'You want me. I know you do.'

'I can't,' she said again. 'You must let me go. I . . .'

'Go where?' he demanded. 'Back to your Romeo?'

'Yes,' she said, shuddering as his hand moved over her, 'yes, my fiancé . . . Please, don't . . .'

'Does he make you feel the way I do?' His mouth dipped to hers again, searing her with his passion, branding her with desire. He lifted his head and stared into her eyes. 'Does he?' he demanded.

Forgive me, Alan, she thought. 'No,' she said in a whisper so low that she hoped only the ocean would hear it. His smile was a trophy of her submission, but before he could kiss her again Paige put her hands against his chest and struggled in his embrace. 'But I'm not going to do this,' she said. 'I . . .'

'You don't want him, Juliet. You want me. You want me to make love to you, here, on the beach.'

'No,' she whispered, but even she could hear the lie trapped in the word. 'No,' she said again, but his arms were holding her tightly, and the stars were beginning to swirl all around her. The moon had climbed higher, casting a silver highway across the black water and a billion stars glittered in the sky. They were the last people on Earth, and love was an imperative. A tremor raced through her. 'Please,' she whispered, 'please . . .'

'Please, what?' he said, and his lips brushed hers. 'Tell me what you want me to do, Juliet. Show me.'

Her head fell back as his lips fround her throat, and she moaned softly as she felt the silky glide of his tongue caress her skin. He was bending her back over his arm, lowering her to the sand, and it was what she wanted. He was what she wanted, he was all she wanted, he was everything . . .

'. . . are you out here?'

No! The voice was recognisable, even if the words were muffled by the surf. Paige stiffened in the stranger's arms.

'It's my mother!'

Her whisper was frantic. He said nothing, and she thought he hadn't understood her. Then she heard his stifled oath and felt the sudden tension in his muscles.

'Keep quiet and she'll go away,' he murmured against her cheek.

'She won't do that,' Paige whispered. 'Let me go—please.'

His eyes burned into hers. 'Only if you swear you'll come back to me.'

Paige shook her head. 'No, no, I can't. I . . .'

'. . . are you?' came her mother's voice.

'She's going to come down here,' Paige said in a desperate whisper. 'Let go of me, I beg you.'

His hands bound her to him. 'Tell me you'll come back,' he said fiercely.

'I can't. I . . .' Paige looked up. Her mother stood silhouetted at the head of the path that led down to the beach. 'All right,' she said breathlessly. 'All right, I'll come back.'

His hands clasped her shoulders, biting into her flesh until she winced. 'Swear it,' he said in an urgent whisper. 'Swear it, or I'll come with you now. I'll tell you mother and your Romeo that you're mine tonight.'

'I'm not. I . . .'

His mouth took hers in a hard, swift kiss that stole her breath away. 'Don't lie to yourself, Juliet. I don't understand it, either, but I know sure as hell that something's happened. And I'm damned if I'm going to let you walk out of my life until I figure it out. Do you understand?'

Paige's heart tumbled crazily. 'Yes,' she whispered, and an overwhelming sense of joy filled her. 'Yes,' she said again, and then she heard her mother's footsteps on the gravel. She touched the man's cheek and then stepped swiftly on to the path. 'I'm here, Mother,' she called.

'For heaven's sake, dear,' her mother said, taking a step towards her. 'We were worried half to death. Where have you been?'

Paige hurried up the last few yards and looped her arm through her mother's, drawing her back towards the gardens and the brightly lit Club house.

'I was . . . I was walking on the beach, Mother. I'm sorry if I worried you.'

'Well, not just me, Paige,' Janet Gardiner said as they moved across the flagstones. 'We were all upset. Your father, Alan—whatever got into you? Were you out here all by yourself?'

Paige glanced over her shoulder. There was only darkness behind her. 'Yes, of course. I'm really sorry. I just . . . I just needed some time to myself, I guess.'

Her mother's footsteps slowed. 'Are you sure you're all right, dear? There's something about you this evening . . .'

'Mother, where's Alan?'

'Looking for you, of course. He . . .'

'I have to talk to him,' Paige said in a rush. 'I have to tell him that this . . .'

Her mother put her arm around Paige's waist. 'Alan understands,' she said soothingly. 'He knows it's just last-minute nerves.'

'Mother, please . . .'

'All brides feel that way. You'll be fine the day of the wedding. Once you see your bridesmaids and the ushers, the flowers, the guests smiling at you, and Alan waiting at the altar—you'll see. All the jitters will vanish.'

It was a litany designed to comfort, but it was also a reminder of reality and responsibility. Paige came to an abrupt halt.

'Will they?' she asked in a whiper.

Janet Gardiner smiled. 'Of course,' she said, and then, looking into Paige's eyes, her smile turned to a worried frown. 'Unless you have real reservations, Paige. Do you? If you're not sure . . .'

Paige caught her lower lip between her teeth. 'Yes. No. God, Mother, I . . . I don't feel . . . I don't feel the way I should about Alan, do you know what I mean? I . . . I just don't feel that way . . .'

Her mother's eyebrows rose. 'The way you felt about that man in New York, you mean.' Her voice was stiff with distaste. 'Is that what you're saying?'

Paige took a breath. 'I'm not comparing the two situations, Mother. I . . .'

'I should hope not. Alan will never hurt you, Paige. You

should be happy.'

'I am happy. I mean, I thought I was. But . . .'

The door ahead of them swung open suddenly, and the noise and smoky warmth of the ballroom spilled over them. Alan gave a sigh of relief as he stepped on to the terrace.

'There you are,' he said. 'What happened to you, sweetheart?'

'I was . . . I was walking, Alan. I . . .'

He put his arm around her shoulders. 'Are you OK?'

Paige nodded. 'Fine.'

'I looked everywhere for you. In the cloakroom, in the car . . .'

'You didn't look on the beach,' Janet Gardiner said. 'That's where she was, Alan. Walking off a bad set of nerves.'

Paige flushed. 'Mother, for heaven's sake . . .'

Alan grinned. 'Terrific. I'm the one who's supposed to be jittery, remember? That's the bridegroom's prerogative.'

Paige drew in her breath. 'Are you?' she whispered.

Alan put his hands on her shoulders and looked into her eyes. 'We're going to be happy,' he said softly. 'I promise.'

Paige stared at her fiancé. They *would* be happy, she thought. Of course they would. What she'd felt a few moments ago, in the arms of a stranger, wasn't happiness. She knew that as well as anyone. Better, perhaps . . .

'Mr and Mrs Fowler have asked us to their house for coffee, dear,' her mother said. 'I'll just get your father and we'll meet you out front.'

Alan smiled as Paige's mother bustled away. 'You're going to get coffee and cake and the whole Fowler clan,' he said teasingly. 'Aunt Dorothy wants to meet you. And Uncle Sam. And what looks like an endless line of cousins.' He bent and kissed her. 'I'm glad your mother found you, sweetheart. We don't want to disappoint them, do we?'

'No, of course not.'

She gave him a quick smile as he clasped her hand in his and led her through the Club house to the front portico. How long would the man on the beach wait for her? she wondered. Five minutes? Ten? Would he be disappointed or angry or . . .

'Here we are, children. Alan, why don't you ask the attendant to get the car?' Her mother took her aside as Alan and her father stepped towards the kerb. 'Stop worrying,' she whispered. 'It's just last-minute nerves, that's all. Three days from now, when you're Mrs Alan Fowler, you'll remember how you felt tonight and you'll laugh.'

Paige nodded and murmured something appropriate. But as she stepped into her fiance's car and let the commitments and obligations of her new life swallow her, she knew that her mother was wrong.

She would remember this night, but she would never laugh. The memories of it would be too bittersweet.

But then, fantasy often was.

CHAPTER THREE

'PAIGE? Paige, have you seen that spray of silk baby's breath I was going to sew on to your head-dress?'

Paige, who had been rummaging in her wardrobe for the mate to the silver pump she held in her hand, sat back on her heels and sighed.

'No, Mother,' she called. 'But I wouldn't worry about it. The head-dress looks lovely just as it is.'

Janet Gardiner stepped into her daughter's room and poked through the lacy garments strewn across the dresser.

'Did I mix it into this lingerie by mistake?' she muttered, and then she sighed and answered her own question. 'No, there's nothing here but lingerie for your trousseau.' The older woman looked at her daughter. 'Haven't you finished packing, dear? The wedding's tomorrow, and you and Alan will have to leave for the airport by five, the latest.'

Paige rose to her feet. 'There's plenty of time, Mother. I'll do the rest tonight, after we get back from the rehearsal dinner.' A frown creased her forehead. 'If we get to it in the first place,' she said, tossing the silver shoe on the bed. 'I can't find the mate to this anywhere.'

'Isn't that . . . yes, there it is,' her mother said, plucking the missing pump from the floor. She looked around the room, smiling at the open suitcases and wardrobes. 'I'm going to miss all this,' she said softly.

Paige laughed as she slipped the shoes on her feet. 'Miss this mess? Come on, Mother. I know you—you can hardly wait to get at this room and clean it.'

Janet Gardiner smiled. 'You know what I mean, dear. I'm

going to miss opening the door and finding you here.' She watched as her daughter smoothed down the skirt of her long blue dress and peered critically at her reflection in the mirror. 'It's hard to believe you'll be Mrs Alan Fowler by this time tomorrow.'

For a fragile moment, Paige's features clouded, and then she returned her mother's smile.

'Look on the bright side, Mother. You'll be able to turn my bedroom back into a guest-room again.'

The older woman laughed. 'It was never anything but your bedroom, Paige, even when you lived in New York City.' She started from the room, then turned and popped her head into the doorway. 'Are you all right?' she asked softly.

Paige nodded. There was a sudden lump in her throat, and she didn't trust herself to try and say anything in return. Instead, she smiled and blew a kiss to her mother, and then she turned away, snatched up the stack of lingerie from the dresser, and put it into one of the open suitcases. When she glanced up again, her mother was gone.

The tremulous smile faded and she sank to the edge of the bed that had been hers since childhood. Tears hung on her lashes and she blinked them back angrily. No more tears, she told herself. She had done enough weeping the past two days to last a lifetime. All brides were edgy—everyone said so—and some were tearful, but God only knew what Alan's family thought of her after the other night. She'd shaken a lot of hands at the Fowler home after they'd left the Hunt Club, and kissed a lot of cheeks, and she'd kept wondering if her smile felt as forced as it looked, until finally Alan had put his arm around her, announced that his bride-to-be was exhausted, and taken her home.

'Are you sure you're OK?' he'd asked when they reached her house.

And Paige had nodded and smiled and assured him that she was fine. 'I'm just tired,' she'd said briskly. 'That's all.'

What else could she have said? she thought now as she sat in her bedroom and stared blindly at the pink and white papered wall ahead. Could she have told him she'd almost given herself to a nameless stranger on a windswept beach? All the time she'd been smiling at Alan's relatives, she'd been thinking about the man, wondering if his heart was as filled with anguish as hers. Was he cursing the cruelty of a Fate that had brought them together and then torn them apart? Or had he just gone back to the Club house and found another woman who'd gone willingly into the night with him, a woman he'd whispered to and caressed, a woman he'd made love to as he'd almost made love to her.

That was the most likely script of all. He'd been looking for an adventure, and he'd found her. She'd made a fool of herself with a stranger, and she should have been grateful it had gone no further than a few moonlight kisses.

Then why was her heart so filled with longing, her dreams so filled with a man whose eyes were the colour of the sea?

'Paige!' Startled, she looked up. 'Alan will be here soon,' her mother said from the doorway. 'And you're not half ready.'

She smiled brightly. 'I will be, Mother. You'll see.'

Her mother laughed. 'That's what you used to say when you were just a little girl.' She hurried across the room and gave her daughter a quick hug, and then she dabbed briskly at her eyes. 'I'm going to ruin my make-up if I keep this up. And then I'll have to redo it, and your father will be furious.' She paused in the doorway and smiled. 'We're going to miss you, dear. It's been lovely, having you live with us this past year.'

Paige met her mother's eyes in the mirror. 'I've been happy here, too.'

Her smile faded as her mother left the room and closed the door behind her. Her mother always made it sound as if she'd simply decided, on impulse, to move back to Connecticut from New York a year ago, but it hadn't been that simple. She'd come home unannounced, the taste of freedom bitter in her mouth. A taxi had taken her from the railway station in Greenwich to the grey-shingled house she'd grown up in. She could still remember taking out her key to open the door, then hesitating, remembering suddenly that she'd not lived here for the past four years, not since she'd turned twenty and finished business school. Slowly, she'd dropped the kay back into her shoulder-bag, and then she'd rung the doorbell.

Janet Gardiner had answered the door, her face showing first delighted surprise and then worried concern as she became aware of her daughere's drawn features. But she'd acted as if Paige's presence were nothing but an unexpected pleasure, bustling her out of her coat and into the kitchen, setting another place at the old oak table before the fireplace, keeping up a line of chatter designed to put her daughter at ease. Her father had arrived home late from the office. To Paige's surprise, he'd hardly seemed to notice her.

'Paige has come for a visit,' her mother said, her eyebrows raised in warning that he ask no questions of their only child.

But her father seemed too absorbed in his own thoughts to do anything more than mumble a few words.

'That's nice,' he said, and then he went off to his study and left the two women to themselves.

'Is something wrong with Father?' Paige asked.

'Nothing more than the usual,' her mother said patiently. 'You know how he is—there's always some pie-in-the-sky scheme hatching in his head that's going to make him an instant millionaire.'

Paige shook her head. 'Poor Daddy. What was it last time? Gold mines or something?'

Mrs Gardiner smiled wearily. 'Or something. I'll never understand how a man who handles money for a firm like Fowlers' can have such bad judgement with his own.' She sighed. 'After the last disaster, I made him promise he wouldn't touch our savings again.'

Paige smiled. 'Does he still say, "no risk, no gain"?'

'Yes. And I told him that was all right as long as you could afford to lose the money you risked.' Her mother laughed. 'Let him squander his cigar money, if it makes him happy. He's a good man, darling, he just thinks we need more—that he's less a man, somehow, because he hasn't been able to give us the moon. I mean, it's not as if he drank or didn't love me . . .' Her eyebrows rose as Paige's face suddenly crumpled. 'Sweetheart, what is it?'

And Paige told her. Not everything; it had all been too recent and too painful. But she told her mother enough. How she'd met someone, thought she was in love, succumbed to her own burgeoning sexuality and found disappointment instead of fulfilment. In one brief encounter, she'd lost both her innocence and her desire.

'And the man?' Her mother touched her hand.

'He said I wasn't a woman. He said . . .'

Her mother put her arms around her. 'Forget about him,' she said fiercely. 'A man like that . . .' Janet Gardiner had looked at her for a long moment, and then she'd smiled. 'I have a wonderful idea,' she'd said, and then she'd made the suggestion that had been destined to change Paige's life. 'Why don't you move back here for a while? You could commute into the city, if you really want to keep that job of yours.'

'Or I could look for one right here in Greenwich,' Paige had said, too quickly, and both women had laughed, Paige with tears glistening in her eyes. 'I was hoping you'd ask me to stay.'

Her mother had patted her hand. 'This is your home, Paige. Of course we want you to stay. And you'll put all this behind you, believe me.'

And she had, Paige thought, staring blindly at the mirror that hung on the wall opposite her bed. First had come the job at Maywalk's department store. And then her father had begun playing Cupid, inviting his boss's son home to dinner, urging her to accept Alan's invitations, mixing together business and social occasions so that she was in Alan's company even when she wasn't dating him.

Not that she hadn't liked him—no one would ever dislike Alan Fowler, with his looks and his charm. And if there were no sparks when he kissed her—well, that was all the better, wasn't it? Compatibility and respect were the soils in which love grew. Passion? Passion was for the movies and for books. It was overrated and oversold, and what she'd experienced of it was enough to last her a lifetime.

Until two nights ago. Until she'd behaved like a . . . a wanton with a man who'd probably disappeared into the night.

And thank goodness he had, she thought as she brushed furiously at her pale blonde hair. At least she wouldn't have to worry about seeing him again. As for the emotions he'd unleashed—she'd learn to feel all that, and more, with Alan. He would be her husband and she'd learn to want his kisses and caresses.

There was a soft tap at the door. 'Alan's here,' her mother said brightly. 'Ready, dear?'

Paige took a deep breath. 'Yes, I'm ready,' she said, and she told herself that she finally was.

The rehearsal dinner as well as the wedding were to be held at the Fowler home. Paige's mother had protested at first, saying that it was the bride's family who should make the wedding, but Alan's mother had been pleasantly but firmly insistent. Alan had urged Paige to go along with his mother's plans. 'It's easier to go along with Mother once she has a bee in her bonnet,' he'd said with a wry smile.

But, in the end, it was Paige's father who'd forced the decision.

'Let the Fowlers do it all,' he'd said. 'They're the ones with the money.' Paige had looked at him in surprise, and he'd given her a quick smile that had barely softened the harshness of his words. 'I only meant that it's foolish to argue.' In the end, Paige and her mother had agreed.

Now, standing in the Fowlers' impressive sitting-room, gazing around her at the milling crowd, Paige was glad they had. It looked as if half the world was present—or half Connecticut and New York, anyway.

'If the Fowlers invited so many people to the rehearsal dinner, just imagine how many there'll be at the wedding tomorrow,' she whispered to her mother. 'I don't think I recognise a dozen faces!'

'Don't worry about a thing, dear. Just smile and say "thank you" and "no, thank you" in all the right places.'

Paige laughed. 'I won't let Alan out of my sight, once he shows up.'

'Shows up, indeed. Where's he gone to?'

'The airport. I only half heard the story. Some last-minute arrival's just come in, and apparently Alan was so delighted to hear about it that he decided to fetch him himself.'

'The mysterious brother, perhaps?'

Paige shrugged. 'Maybe. All I know is I've been left here to hold down the fort. Believe me,' she laughed, 'Alan's going to pay for . . . oh, God!'

The words were a choked whisper. Her mother turned to her in surprise.

'Paige? What is it? You're white as a sheet.'

'I . . . nothing. Nothing. I just . . .'

Paige could hear herself stammering, saying words that made no sense. But it was a miracle she could speak at all, she thought, staring across the crowded room. He was here. The stranger, the man she'd let make love to her two nights before—he was here, a guest in the Fowler home, a guest at her rehearsal dinner. He hadn't seen her yet; he was standing at the far end of the room, alone, holding a glass in his hand. She watched as someone stopped beside him—a woman, young, lovely, her face tilted smilingly up to his. He nodded, said something, but there was no answering smile. The woman spoke again, saying something else, but he seemed to be barely listening.

'Paige, will you please answer me? What's wrong?'

She drew her gaze from him and looked at her mother. 'I ... nothing,' she said carefully. 'I just thought I saw ... I saw someone went to school with, that's all. Someone I ... I never dreamed I'd see again.' *Smile,* she told herself fiercely. But, when she did, her lips felt glued to her teeth.

Her mother put her hand to her heart and laughed. 'You gave me quite a start, dear. I thought you'd seen a ghost. Well, why don't you go over and say hello? I'll just go find Mrs Fowler.' She laughed again. 'Maybe our handful of guests has shown up and we won't feel so outnumbered.'

'Yes, fine. I'll just ... I'll find you in a few minutes, Mother.'

By then, I'll have thought up some excuse for leaving ... But that would only postpone the inevitable. If he was here tonight, it was likely he'd be at the wedding tomorrow. What to do, what to do? What if she simply walked up to him, offered her apologies for her disreputable behaviour? What if she begged for his silence, for his understanding ...

He'd seen her! Paige's heart stood still. Everything around her faded as the man's eyes met hers. His face grew dark, his lips narrow. The woman beside him was still talking, still smiling, and suddenly he shoved his glass into her hand and brushed past her. Paige knew, as surely as she knew he was coming straight for her, that he would never accept either her apologies or her pleas for understanding.

But he wouldn't make a scene, not in front of all these people. No, she told herself, no, he wouldn't ... She watched as he moved rapidly through the crowd, rudely shouldering people out of his way if they didn't step aside quickly enough. His eyes were locked on her face, unwavering pools of icy fire. The first image she'd had of him returned to her, and her pulse began to race. Tonight, the lion had no intention of waiting for the wildebeest to come near. He was the killer—and she was his prey.

How could she have let herself think he wouldn't make a scene? He was capable of anything—her heart thudded into her throat and she turned wildly and began to run. She heard a peal of nervous laughter as she spun past surprised faces. She thought fleetingly of how impossible it was going to be to try and explain this to Alan. But she had seen the savagery in the stranger's eyes, and all that mattered at this moment was getting away from him. She fled from the sitting-room, into the darkness of the rest of the house, trying to remember where the rear door led.

He caught her just as she was half-way through it. She tried to slam the door in his face, but he was far too strong for her. The door glanced off his shoulder, and then he was past it, reaching for her, grasping her by the shoulders with hands that bit into her flesh like talons.

'Let go of me!' she gasped, trying to twist free of him. 'Damn you . . .'

He kicked the door closed. 'Did you really think you could get away from me?' His voice was low and filled with rage.

'I told you to let go of me. How dare you treat me like this? I . . .'

'Shut up,' he said, slipping his arm around her shoulders.

She struggled against him as he began to draw her away from the house. 'Where are you taking me?' she demanded. 'I . . .'

'I'm taking you to the summer-house,' he said grimly, half lifting her dragging feet from the ground. 'I don't need a whole damned houseful of people out here staring at me.'

'It's a little late to worry about that, don't you think? A few minutes ago . . .'

'You're the one who ran,' he said, pulling her up the wooden steps that led into the trellised gazebo that stood far to the rear of the Fowler lawn.

'Of course I ran. You looked as if you . . . as if you . . .'

He grasped her shoulders with a roughness that made her gasp. 'As if what?' he growled, staring down at her.

Paige swallowed drily. The trees scattered about the lawn had been strung with coloured lights for the party, mottling his face with reds, blues, and yellows.

'As if . . . as if you wanted to kill me,' she whispered finally.

His mouth twisted. 'I thought about it, believe me. The other night, when I finally let myself believe you'd left . . .'

'Look, about that—about the other night . . .'

His eyes darkened. 'Did you have a good time playing with me, Juliet?'

Colour flooded her cheeks. 'You're a fine one to talk about games,' she hissed. 'I wasn't the one who started things. It was you . . .'

The words caught in her throat as he shook her. 'I waited on that God-forsaken beach for an hour, damn you! And then I went back to the Club house—and you weren't there.' His hands slid from her shoulders and a weariness crept into his voice. 'I couldn't even ask anybody where you'd gone—hell, I didn't even know your name.'

Paige ran her tongue over her lips. 'I . . . I'm sorry,' she whispered. 'I didn't mean . . .'

She flinched as he spun towards her. 'Didn't you? Then what the hell was all that about, Juliet?' He caught her by the arms and stared into her eyes. 'Or is that just something you do when you go to parties, hmm? Have a drink, have a canapé, have a dance—and then go off with some man and drive him half out of his mind with wanting you and . . .'

'Don't you dare talk that way to me! You have no right.'

'Don't I? You made a fool out of me. You . . .'

'I tried to tell you it was no good, but you wouldn't listen. I kept saying I had to go back to my fiancé, but you . . . you . . .'

To her horror, Paige felt tears fill her eyes and begin to

slide down her cheeks. It was bad enough that he'd made a fool of her the other night; she didn't have to let this man reduce her to tears. Quickly, she brushed the back of her hand across her lashes and turned away.

'Just let go of me,' she whispered.

'And where the hell do you think you're going now?'

'Let go of me. Please.'

His hands moved gently to her shoulders, and he turned her stiff, unyielding body towards his.

'Don't cry,' he said fiercely. 'Dammit, Juliet . . .'

Paige lifted her face to him, the tears glistening damply on her lashes, and with a whispered oath, he pulled her into his arms and kissed her. It was a kiss that told her, more clearly than words, that his torment these past days had been as great as hers. There was passion in it and desire, there was anger and tenderness—but underlying all there was an awareness that this one kiss would not, could not, be enough.

'Juliet, Juliet,' he murmured against her lips, 'why didn't you come back to me?'

Her arms slid around his neck. 'I couldn't,' she whispered. 'I couldn't . . . and I can't stay with you now.'

His arms tightened around her. 'Don't say that,' he growled. She moaned as his hand moved over her, cupping the fullness of her breast, sliding across her hip, curving across her buttocks. 'I'm not letting you go,' he said against her throat. 'Not this time.'

He moved her against him, bringing her body tightly against his, and she felt the heated strength of him press into her.

'You must,' she whispered. 'Please. My fiancé . . .'

He laughed throatily. 'Are we going to talk about him again? What kind of man is he, this fiancé of yours?' His hand moved over her, possessively claiming each curve. 'You don't want him, Juliet. You know you don't.'

Paige closed her eyes. 'No,' she murmured. 'Not . . . not this way. But . . .'

'He's never made you feel like this, Juliet.' His lips moved along her cheek, to her throat. 'Spend the night with me,' he whispered. 'Let me show you how it can be with us.'

'I can't, don't you understand? It's too late. My fiancé . . .'

He drew back and looked down at her. 'What is it like when you're with him?'

Paige's cheeks flamed. 'I . . . I . . .'

He lifted her left hand and brought it to his lips. 'Is it like that diamond you wear? Is the fire locked away inside the cold stone?'

'You mustn't say things like that. He . . .'

'I'm only telling you what we both know,' he said. His hands slipped from her shoulders. The party lights danced on the ruby ring he wore, and she watched as he slipped it from his fingers. 'Give me your hand.' Her eyes scanned his face and then, slowly, she did as he'd asked. He took her hand in his and placed the ring on her palm. 'A man who would give you a diamond doesn't really want you, Juliet,' he said softly.

Paige stared at the ring he'd given her. The ruby glowed against her skin like a burning coal, its antique setting intricate and exquisite. She looked from it to him and shook her head.

'I . . . I don't understand.'

'You're like the blood ruby in that ring,' he said softly, cupping her face in his hands and raising it to his. 'Rare, precious, burning with passionate life.' Her eyes closed as his mouth took hers. When he raised his head again, his eyes were dark. 'Keep the ring. Look into it tonight, into the flame that blazes in its heart, and think of me and of how it will be when we're together.' His hand closed over hers, and she felt the heat of the ruby sear her palm. 'Cherish the flame in your dreams, Juliet, and tomorrow, when I see you again . . .'

'Tomorrow,' she repeated, as if he were speaking an unknown language.

'The wedding. You'll be there, won't you?'

'I . . . yes, yes, I'll be there.'

'We'll spend the day together,' he said, and he smiled at her. 'We'll do all the things people do when they first meet. We'll talk and we'll joke . . .' The smile faded, and he put his arms around her. 'And then I'll take you in my arms and I'll kiss you, like this.' His lips moved slowly, teasingly, over hers. 'And then I'll ask you to come with me. 'And . . .'

Tomorrow!

'Please,' Paige said desperately, 'you've got to listen. I . . .'

'If you tell me "no", I'll go away and you'll never see me again.' His arms tightened as he gathered her closer. 'But you won't,' he said, his voice a whisper that slid along her skin. 'You won't, Juliet. You'll look into my eyes and say you want me to make love to you.'

'You don't understand. Tomorrow . . .'

There was the sound of a door slamming closed, and then a whistle pierced the night.

'Hey, are you guys out here?'

Dear God! It was Alan. Paige's heart began to race. 'You've got to get out of here,' she hissed. 'Please!'

'Paige? Where are you, sweetheart?'

'Don't you hear me? Dammit—that's Alan. That's my fiancé . . .'

The man's eyes darkened, narrowed, until they were pinpoints of cobalt fire. His hands grasped her shoulders, his fingers biting into her until she gasped with pain.

'I tried to tell you,' she whispered. 'I . . .'

The look on his face silenced her. 'I ought to kill you,' he said softly. 'Jesus, I'd like to put my hands around your throat and . . .'

There was a clatter of footsteps on the gazebo stairs, and an arm slid around her waist.

'There you are, sweetheart,' Alan said, smiling at her. Paige's eyes widened as he threw his other arm loosely around the stranger's neck. 'Terrific!' he said happily. 'I see you two have already met. Well, Quinn, what do you think of her? What does my big brother have to say about my blushing bride?'

CHAPTER FOUR

WEDDING days were supposed to be storybook perfect. Blue skies, bright sun, not a cloud in the sky. And that was the way this one had dawned, Paige thought as she stood looking out her bedroom window. The few remaining leaves on the old maple tree gleamed gold and scarlet. When she was little, she'd loved to scramble into the tree's low, curving branches and sit safely hidden from the world in its leafy embrace.

If only she could do that now—climb into the maple and put her arms around the rough, scarred wood, hide there until this terrible day was over. But she wasn't a child any more, and there was no escaping reality. Paige sighed and took the last, bitter sip from a cup of cold coffee. The only thing she could hope for now was a modicum of kindness from Alan. He hadn't called yet, but he would—after Quinn had told him everything.

Somehow, she'd lived through last night, through the awful moment at the gazebo, murmuring some nonsense about the surprise of meeting Quinn at last, all the while waiting for him to denounce her. But he'd been silent, watching her with a terrifying intensity, then muttering some polite phrases similar to hers. Alan had smiled and then they'd all returned to the house together, Alan walking happily between them.

Paige's mother had come to her rescue when they entered the sitting-room. 'Your hair needs fixing,' she'd said, and she'd hustled Paige off to the safety of the downstairs bathroom. 'Where on earth did you run off to?' she'd demanded as soon as the door closed. Paige had attempted a mumbled excuse, but her mother had waved it off. 'You've been acting very strangely, Paige. I keep telling everyone it's just last-minute jitters, but—are you all right?'

It struck Paige that her mother had asked her that same question more and more in the past few days. She'd lied again, of course, saying yes, she was fine. What else could she have said? she thought now, staring blindly at the old maple. She couldn't have told her the truth—that, even as they spoke, Quinn was probably telling Alan that his fianceée was a . . . a . . .

Paige's empty coffee-cup clattered as she put it down. A thin beam of sunlight reflected from the diamond on her finger. Alan's ring, she thought, and her hand went to the valley between her breasts. Quinn's blood ruby lay warm against her skin, suspended on a thin golden chain. What perversity had made her put it on?

She glanced at the clock beside her bed. The wedding was just a few hours away. Why hadn't Alan called? Surely Quinn had told him by now. All last night, she'd alternately dreaded and welcomed the moment when she'd have to confess her duplicity, but nothing had happened. And Quinn—Quinn had lurked in the background, his face a mask of darkness, watching her . . .

'Paige.' She looked up as the door opened. 'It's time to dress, dear.'

'Has Alan phoned, Mother?'

Janet Gardiner shook her head. 'He's not supposed to, is he? It's bad luck or something.' She opened the wardrobe and carefully slipped Paige's long-skirted bridal gown from its hanger. 'Isn't it beautiful?' she sighed.

Paige watched as her mother spread the gown on the bed. The yards of hand-made French lace, so lovely and delicate, seemed a mockery.

'Mother? I was wondering—what do you know about

Quinn Fowler?'

'Alan's brother?' Her mother shrugged. 'Not much, only what Mr Fowler told your father. He lives abroad—London, I think. Apparently, he's been a great disappointment to the Fowlers. He left here under some sort of cloud. But he and Alan are still close. Why do you ask?'

Paige swallowed. 'No particular reason. I was just thinking . . .' Her words trailed away. 'Mother? What if—what if something happened and I didn't marry Alan?'

Her mother smiled. 'Nothing's going to happen,' she said gently.

'But just suppose—what if I changed my mind? Would you be upset?'

'Have you changed your mind?' her mother asked after a moment.

Paige shook her head. 'I . . . I'm just asking.'

Janet Gardiner crossed the room and put her arm around her daughter. 'Paige, dear, every bride has last-minute doubts.'

'I know. But . . .'

Her mother's eyes searched hers. 'Do you want to talk about it?' she asked softly.

Paige shook her head again. 'No,' she whispered.

Her mother nodded. 'Do what your heart tells you,' she said, her eyes never leaving her daughter's. 'That's all that matters.'

Tears glistened in Paige's eyes. 'You're a terrific mother,' she said, with a quick smile. 'Have I ever told you that?'

Janet Andrew's eyes were damp as well. 'Not half often enough,' she laughed, and then she kissed Paige's cheek. 'Now,' she said briskly, 'let's get you into this gown, shall we? Time's running out.'

Her mother's words rang through Paige's mind as she stood in the centre of a small upstairs room in the Fowler house.

Time was, indeed, running out. The early sounds of the wedding festivities carried clearly up the rear staircase: the hum of conversation between the caterer and his assistants, the clink of silverware, the discreet tones of Vivaldi. In less than an hour, the house would be filled with people, and she would move slowly down the flower-bedecked main staircase, across the pink and white runner laid over the Aubusson carpet, to Alan's side.

Except that none of that would happen. Any minute now, the door would open and Alan would confront her. Alan and Quinn. And she was alone and ready. There would be no audience to her disgrace.

'Go and see to our guests,' she'd said to her mother. 'You know Mrs Fowler—she'll swallow them alive if you're not there.'

Her father had seemed eager to leave her. 'This is a good thing you're doing,' he'd said, and the remark had seemed so solemn and heavy that it had brought the only smile of the day to Paige's face.

Paige looked at the clock and felt a moment of panic. Was it possible Quinn had changed his mind? Had he decided not to tell Alan anything? Was she less than an hour away from becoming the wife of a man she didn't love, a man she didn't deserve? No, that was out of the question. She'd seen the look on Quinn's face. He hated her and he loved his brother, and . . .

The door opened and slammed shut. *Alan* . . . Heart pounding, Paige spun towards the door. She felt the blood drain from her face. It wasn't Alan—it was Quinn. And he was alone.

'What are you doing here?' she whispered. 'Where's Alan?'

His lips drew away from his teeth. 'What a charming way to greet your brother-in-law,' he said pleasantly, while his eyes moved over her. 'You look lovely, sweet Juliet. So pure and virginal.'

Paige felt a rush of heat to her face. Had there been a way to run from the look of disgust in his eyes, she would have. But she could only square her shoulders and force herself to meet his gaze without flinching.

'Did Alan send you? Is he . . . Has he . . .'

The smile left his face. 'He doesn't know I'm here. He doesn't know anything, Paige. You've done quite a job on my little brother.'

'You mean . . . you haven't told him? But . . .'

'Alan wouldn't believe me if I told him you were the whore of Babylon,' Quinn said harshly. 'God knows, I tried. I took him out for a drink after everyone left last night. Hell, I got as far as saying he was making a mistake when he laughed and slapped me on the back. He said he'd expected me to try and talk him out of getting married. And when I started to say I didn't think you were right for him, he laughed again and told me I was just jealous of his good luck.' His face darkened and his voice fell to a whisper. 'You don't know the effort it took not to tell him his "luck" could have been anybody's at the right place and the right time.'

The accusation pierced her heart. 'It's not true,' she whispered. 'What I did with you . . .'

A sneer curved across his mouth. 'I was there, remember? You had an itch and you needed somebody to scratch it, that's all.' Paige's face turned white and Quinn laughed. 'What's the matter, baby? Is that too vulgar for your delicate ears?'

'You can't talk to me like that,' she said. 'You . . .'

He moved towards her with such an intensity of purpose that she took a step back. But there was no place to go; her shoulders hit the wall just as his hands closed on her arms.

'What was it that got to you, Paige? Weeks of playing the innocent with Alan? No, I guess that wasn't so difficult—he doesn't excite you, does he? You told me that straight off.'

Tears rose to her eyes. 'Quinn, please, it wasn't like that . . .'

He drew her towards him. 'Was it me who excited you, Paige? Or was it the idea of being taken by a stranger that turned you on?'

'Please, Quinn, I beg you . . .'

He stared at her for a long moment, and then he flung her from him. 'God, you're good at what you do,' he muttered. 'No wonder Alan fell for your act, the poor bastard.'

Paige shook her head. 'I never pretended with Alan. I told him . . .'

'The crap I had to listen to last night!' Quinn shook his head in disbelief. 'You sure as hell figured him out fast, Juliet. All you had to do was play it coy, bat those long lashes and say "no" whenever he tried to lay a hand on you, and a marriage proposal was almost guaranteed.'

'It wasn't like that, Quinn. I told Alan I didn't love him.'

'And what a nice touch that was,' he said with a bitter laugh. 'He damned near blushed when he told me he was going to teach you about love.' He bent his head towards her, his eyes filled with hate. 'I'll bet you could write a book about *love*,' he snarled, giving the word an inflection that twisted it into an obscenity. 'Alan must have been a gift from the gods. Your chance at a rich husband—and an insurance policy for your father, all in one neat package.'

Her gaze swung across his face. 'What are you talking about? What's my father got to do with this?'

'Don't try that act on me, baby. It won't work. I know everything.'

'And I don't know what you're talking about, Quinn. My father . . .'

'I've got to admit, you and your old man were clever. Alan never suspected he was being played for a fool.' Quinn let go of her and stalked across the room. 'Jesus, he even told me how grateful he was to your father, how he had needed an ally when you and he first started going out and how it was your father he turned to.'

'My father likes Alan. He . . .'

He spun on his heel and faced her. 'Don't lie to me, dammit!' She drew in her breath as he moved slowly towards her again. 'Whose idea was it, Juliet? Yours or your father's?'

'I . . . I don't know what you're talking about,' she said, her mouth dry with fear.

'Damn, but it was clever! Your father dangled you in front of Alan, you played hard to get, and Alan was drawn deeper and deeper into the web.' He reached out suddenly and grasped her shoulders. 'And once he was caught, the Gardiner father and daughter team had two problems neatly solved.'

'You're crazy, Quinn! I want you to get out of this room. I . . .'

'Problem one,' he said, ignoring her, 'what do you do with a daughter who's been around a little too much? Problem two: what do you do when you've got your hand in the till up to your elbow? Solution? Simple. You tart up your tarnished goods with a fresh coat of paint and marry her off to the man you've been stealing from. Then you've got nothing to worry about. Who'd bring criminal charges against a relative?'

Paige looked at him as if he were speaking gibberish. 'Criminal charges? What are you talking about?'

'I'm talking about your father,' he snapped. 'He's a goddamned thief!'

'My father?' she said incredulously. 'Look, say what you want about me, Quinn. I know what you think of me and I can't . . . I can't blame you. But my father? My father's been chief accountant at Fowler's for years. He . . .'

'He's been stealing from Fowler's for years.'

'You're a liar,' she said quickly, her voice sharp with anger. 'You don't know anything about him. For that matter, you don't know a damned thing about Fowler's, either. You walked away from your family and your responsibilities . . .' The bite of his hands made her breath hiss between her teeth. 'You're hurting me,' she said, trying to twist free. 'Let go of me. Dammit, let go or I'll . . .'

'You'll what?' he said, lifting his hands from her with exaggerated care. 'Call for help?' He laughed. 'Send for the police? That would be rich, wouldn't it? The embezzler's daughter and the cops.'

Paige drew in her breath. 'Embezzler?'

'What's the matter, Paige? Do you think the word's too harsh? That's what he's been doing. Hell, you probably know the story better than I do. Take a little from this account, a little from that—dormant accounts, of course, the kind no one ever looks at twice. Who's going to catch you, especially if you're the man in charge?'

'That's impossible,' she said quickly. 'If anyone did something like that, Alan or his father would have known. Who are you to come out of nowhere and say these things?'

Quinn's mocking smile faded. Suddenly, the room seemed cool.

'I own a consulting firm, Paige. Didn't Alan tell you? Computers, software, programs—my speciality is setting up accounting procedures for firms like Fowler's.' The smile came again, quick and cold. 'When my father heard I was coming home for Alan's wedding, he tossed me a bone. "See what you can do for our records department," he said, probably not expecting much.' His voice dropped to a whisper. 'But I did a great deal. I spent the past few days instituting a computer program that took Fowler's out of the dark ages and into the twenty-first century.'

Paige stared at him. None of what he was saying made

sense. 'But . . . but Alan said you weren't even arriving until . . .'

'Alan was so busy being a bridegroom that he didn't know which end was up.' His eyes narowed. 'I flew in the evening of the Masquerade Ball. Of course, he didn't see me that night. Nobody did, thanks to your little tease on the beach.'

Colour flooded her face. 'That's not the way it was, Quinn.'

'Since then,' he said, ignoring the interruption, 'I've spent every day programming the computers. I turned up your father's little scheme the day before yesterday.' A thin smile spread across his mouth. 'Do you want a good laugh? When I realised who he was—Paige Gardiner's father—I almost went crazy trying to find a way to bury what I'd found. I didn't want Alan and his sweet little bride to learn that her daddy was an embezzler—not right before the wedding.' He looked at her. 'If you don't believe me, find your father and ask him about the Melnick account. See what reaction you get.'

It was all too much. He was as wrong about her father as he was about her. He had to be. Her father, a thief? Never. He wouldn't steal.

No risk, no gain. Her skin chilled, as if the ghosts called up by Quinn's accusations were brushing against her. As a child, she'd overheard more than one hushed, late-night quarrel between her parents. It was always over the same thing—her father's determination to 'make a quick killing'. He was chasing fool's gold, her mother would say, and then a cold silence would settle over the household for days on end.

What if her father's schemes had got out of hand? What if the eccentricity had become addiction? Memories drawn from the past months tumbled through Paige's mind: she thought of the way her father had thrown her at

Alan—there was no pretending he hadn't. And then there were the vaguely unpleasant comments he'd made these past weeks about the Fowlers and their money. Now that she stopped to think, he'd been acting strangely ever since she'd returned home.

'I only want what's best for all of us.'

Wasn't that what her father had said the other night? And she'd laughed and teased him about his choice of words. Suppose it hadn't been a slip of the tongue? Suppose it was an expression of relief that he was going to be related to the Fowlers, protected by marriage from public shame or worse?

She knew, suddenly, that it was all too impossible for Quinn to be lying. What he'd told her was the truth. Panic filled her. Her father was an embezzler. A thief.

'What do you want me to do?' Her voice was desperate. 'I'll do whatever you day, Quinn. Just promise me you won't expose my father.'

His eyes darkened. 'Ah,' he said softly, 'the act is over. No more pretending you don't know what I'm talking about, Paige?' Denial was pointless; her silence was his answer. Quinn nodded. 'All right, your father's little game is over. I'll see to it that it stays buried—if you do as I say.'

She nodded wearily. 'Tell me what you want.'

His voice was sharp. 'I want you out of Alan's life.'

Anger stirred within her. 'You think you know me, Quinn, but you don't. I'd have made your brother a good wife. I . . .'

He laughed in her face. 'A good wife? You mean a scheming wife, don't you, baby? One who would lie cold in his arms, just to keep him on edge, while she slept her way through town.'

Tears gleamed on her lashes. 'There's no point to this conversation,' she said. 'You want me out of his life, and that's fine. I'll tell Alan the wedding's off. I was going to do it days ago . . .'

He laughed again. 'I'll bet you were.'

Her eyes met his. 'Bring Alan to me. I'll tell him I've had second thoughts about marrying him. I'll find a way that won't hurt him.'

'A way that won't tarnish your halo, you mean. Yeah, I can see it now. By the time you're finished, he'll be at your feet, begging you to give him a chance to make you happy.'

Paige caught his sleeve as he paced by. 'Then I'll write him a letter.' Quinn stopped and turned to her, his blue-green eyes on her face, and she hurried on, 'I'll—I'll tell him I can't go through with the wedding. And then I'll leave. Right now. I have my luggage here, even my passport.' She waited, but he said nothing. 'That would work, wouldn't it? I'll go away for a while. You can go back to . . . to wherever it is you came from, and . . .'

Two hard lines etched beside his narrowed mouth. 'Wonderful,' he said softly. His hand snaked out and grasped her wrist, and his voice exploded with rage. 'Do you think all men are fools? I'll leave and you'll return—is that it? And then you'll tell Alan you've had a change of heart, you never should have cancelled the wedding . . .'

Paige shook her head. 'I wouldn't. I swear I wouldn't . . .'

She cried out as his fingers tightened on the fragile bones in her wrist.

'You're hurting me,' she gasped.

'Am I?' he growled, drawing her to him. 'I sure as hell hope so.'

'I didn't lure Alan into anything. He wanted me.'

'Damned right, he wanted you.' His mouth twisted as he leaned closer to her. 'What man wouldn't, once you turned those eyes on him? I should know.'

Her cheeks pinkened. 'You weren't innocent. I didn't seek you out, hunt you down . . .'

Quinn's eyes blazed. 'When a man is interested, Paige, an

honest whore tells him her price first.'

Her hand was a blur as it swung through the air and cracked against his cheek. The sound of flesh striking flesh echoed through the room.

'You son of a bitch,' Paige said in a whisper. Her violet eyes darkened to indigo. 'You know what I'm going to do, Quinn? I'm going to marry Alan, whether you like it or not—and there isn't a damned thing you can do to stop me! You were absolutely right. He'll believe whatever I tell him.'

'He'll believe what the computer print-outs tell him. Your father's a thief.'

'It isn't my father your brother wants,' she said coldly. 'It's me, and he'll take me on any terms—even if they include forgiving my father.'

There was silence, and then Quinn nodded. 'You're good, Paige, but not good enough. You forgot one thing—our little romp on the beach the other night.' He smiled unpleasantly. 'Something tells me Alan won't want you after I tell him about that.'

Her chin rose as her eyes fixed on his. 'If you do,' she said softly, 'I'll have to tell him how you forced yourself on me. How you almost raped me. Who do you think he'll believe then?'

She thought, for an instant, she had pushed him too far. his face darkened, his eyes turned to glass. Paige held her breath, readying herself for his attack. Then, just when she was sure her heart was going to leap from her chest, he did the unexpected. He smiled.

'Sweet, sweet Juliet,' he said, his voice almost a purr. 'Thank you for showing me your true face. It's hard to look into those eyes and remember what a bitch you really are.' His hand flexed more tightly around her wrist. 'You're right— Alan will fall for whatever lies you tell him. And then you and your thieving father will have it all.' Paige said nothing, and Quinn twisted her towards him. 'I'm right, aren't I?'

Her wrist hurt beneath the clutch of his fingers, but not as much as her heart. To think she'd wanted this man to make love to her. To think she'd almost given up the safe haven of Alan's arms . . .

How I hate you!

'Yes,' she said, 'and there's nothing you can do about it. I'm telling you that there's going to be a wedding today.'

He laughed softly. 'You're right.' His arms began to close around her, imprisoning her against him. 'There damned well will be a wedding today. But not in this house. And not between you and Alan.' He paused and a smile touched his lips, never warming the coldness in his eyes. 'You've left me no choice, Paige. There's only one way to stop you. You're going to marry me. You're going to be my wife.'

She stared at him, stunned. Somewhere in the distant reaches of the house, there was loud laughter, and Paige wondered crazily if everyone had heard what Quinn had said and they were all in on the joke.

'Wh . . . what?'

He shifted her against him, and she felt the hardness of his body. Last night, the feel of him against her had made her breathless with desire. Now it terrified her. He smiled, and she knew he'd sensed her fear and drew pleasure from it.

'Leaves you speechless with happiness, doesn't it?' The smile faded, as quickly as a light doused by the flick of a switch. 'There's no other way I can protect my brother from you.'

She stared at him, waiting for the laughter that would tell her he was making some kind of ugly joke, but his eyes were expressionless.

'You . . . you can't be serious . . .'

'Deadly serious, sweet Juliet.'

Her heart began to race. 'I . . . I'd have to be crazy to marry you.'

Quinn cocked his head. 'Or desperate,' he said softly. 'How far will you go to save your father from prison?'

'You wouldn't . . .'

He grinned. 'Wouldn't I? The guests are down there waiting. All I have to do is walk up to the altar and make a brief announcement. "Good afternoon, everyone," I'll say. "I'm afraid the wedding will be cancelled. You see, the bride's father is an embezzler, and I've had to telephone for the police. The bride's asked me to tell you the groom will marry her anyway, at which time the groom's parents, not wanting to have a thief in the family, will disown him and announce his dismissal from the firm. I'm sorry if this has spoiled your day, but just think of what it's done for the bride and her daddy." '

'You bastard,' she said softly.

'What a colourful vocabulary you have, Paige. Alan would be shocked to hear such words fall from that soft mouth.'

'Don't you care about hurting Alan?'

Quinn shrugged her words away. 'Being married to you would hurt him more.'

'He'd hate you. Your whole family would hate you. They . . .'

His lips drew back in a cold smile. 'I've survived worse.'

She made a last, desperate try. 'Alan will still want me, Quinn. He'll try to win me back.'

'Give it up,' he said softly. 'Once you belong to me, any man who wants to stay healthy won't look at you twice, including my little brother.' His eyes moved over her face, to the gentle curve of her breast barely visible above the lace neckline of her bridal gown, and then he looked into her eyes again. 'You wanted a Fowler and you've got one.' A smile twisted his lips. 'Believe me, Paige, the one you got is the one you deserve.'

Her heart fluttered in panic. 'You can't do this,' she whispered. 'The wedding's going to start soon. Everyone's waiting. Quinn, please, you have to listen to me. Your parents . . . my parent . . .'

'Don't forget the compensations, Paige.'

When she saw what was in his eyes, she began to struggle against him, but his strength overwhelmed her. He drew her to him and his mouth captured hers in a kiss that was a brutal message of dominance. There was no softness, no seeking warmth. His kiss was meant to establish the boundaries of their relationship. She was his. He would own her, and there was nothing she could do about it.

'Do you understand me?'

Paige put her hand to her mouth and wiped it clean. 'How could I ever have wanted you to touch me?' she whispered.

Tears filled her eyes and slid down her cheeks. Something flickered in the depths of his aquamarine eyes, but it was gone as swiftly as it had come.

'I want to be out of the door in five minutes,' he said curtly. 'Change out of that gown while I write a note to Alan. I'll dictate notes for you to write to him and your parents. I'll make it sound as if we couldn't help ourselves. They'll think we can't live without each other.' His smile sent a chill through her blood. 'It's almost the truth, in a twisted sort of way, isn't it, Juliet?'

'Dear lord, how I hate you!'

'Maybe the judge who marries us can work those words into the wedding vows. Believe me, the feeling is mutual.'

Their eyes met and locked, and then Quinn pushed her from him.

'Change your clothing,' he snapped. 'Make it fast.'

She looked at him helplessly. 'Turn your back.'

Quinn laughed. 'A modest bride. Just what I've always

wanted.'

But he did as she'd asked. And, when she was dressed in what was to have been her going-away outfit, Paige slid Alan's diamond from her finger and placed it gently on the table.

Beneath her silk blouse, Quinn's ruby still warmed her flesh.

CHAPTER FIVE

PAIGE watched as Quinn took a pen and paper from the desk. *Dear Alan* . . . He wrote the words in a strong, firm hand. A shudder ran through her and she turned away.

This couldn't be happening. Surely it was a dream from which she'd soon awaken? But the scratch of pen across paper was a real as the sight of her bridal gown lying in a discarded heap across the bed. She watched as Quinn finished the first page of the letter and began the next. God, there had to be a way to stop him! He couldn't really do this to her—he wouldn't. He . . .

No, of course he wouldn't. This was a trick, that was all. Quinn wanted to be certain she'd fade from his brother's life for ever. This was only a melodrama to ensure that she did.

Her desperate hope died as soon as Quinn finished writing. He looked up and shoved the letter towards her.

'Sign it,' he said.

She looked at him blankly. 'Quinn, you . . . you can't really mean . . .'

His eyes raked her with cold fire. 'Have you changed your mind, Paige? Would you prefer I go downstairs and make my announcement?'

She shook her head. 'No. But . . .'

'Sign the letter, Paige.'

She took a step towards him and picked up the letter. Her hands trembled as she read the words she and Quinn had supposedly written together.

Words seemed to leap from the page. 'By the time you

64

read this . . . can't go through with our wedding . . . don't want to hurt you . . . always care for you but I've fallen in love with Quinn . . .'

'You said I could write to Alan myself.'

His smile was curt. 'I changed my mind. Let's go, Paige. Sign it.'

The paper trembled and fell from her hand. Quinn picked it up and thrust it at her.

'Do it,' he growled.

'Quinn . . .' Her voice broke. 'Quinn, please—I beg you. Don't force me into this. I swear I won't marry Alan. I don't love him—I never did. And my father . . . maybe he can explain. Maybe . . .'

His eyes were bottomless and dark. 'Maybe he can grow old in prison. Sign the note, Paige.'

His voice was soft. She read the threat in his eyes and then she took the paper from him and scrawled her name alongside his.

'You have two minutes to write to your parents.' His mouth twisted. 'Not that your old man will give a damn. As long as you marry the Fowler who can guarantee his safety.'

Paige addressed her note to both her mother and her father, but the words were directed to Janet Gardiner. She built on the advice her mother had given her earlier that morning: it made for an effective lie.

'I've fallen in love with . . .' Her hand paused, trembling, and Quinn laughed. 'Write my name, Juliet. You may as well get used to it.' Paige took a deep breath. '. . . with someone else,' she wrote. 'I've done as you said, Mother, and followed my heart.'

Quinn's breath was warm on her cheek as he read over her shoulder. 'That's it,' he said. 'There won't be a dry eye in the house after that's made the rounds.'

That was when she'd first begun to believe that he might really take her away with him. The pulse that beat in the hollow of her throat leaped to the sudden pounding of her blood. She wiped her damp palms along the silk skirt of her going-away suit, watching as Quinn pulled off his dark grey morning-jacket and tossed it aside.

'What are you doing?' she whispered.

His fingers flew along the studs on his starched shirt. 'Changing my clothes. This used to be my room—there should be something I can wear left in the wardrobe.' His voice grew muffled. 'Here we go,' he said, flashing her a mirthless grin as he tossed a corduroy suit on the bed. 'It's probably going to be a tight fit, but it's better than walking around New York City on a weekend morning, wearing a swallowtail coat.'

He shrugged off his shirt and tossed it after the jacket. His chest and shoulders were naked, and Paige's glance skimmed across his torso, refusing to see, yet fascinated by, the dark, curling hair that covered his chest, and the well-defined muscles in his arms and shoulders. His eyes caught hers and she flushed and turned away.

'New York?'

Quinn grunted and she heard the hiss of metal. 'New York,' he repeated. 'And then London.'

London. Of course—that was where he lived. If he was really planning on going through with this, that was where he'd take her. She swallowed past the nervous laughter that rose in her throat. Alan had apologised a dozen times for having to rush her off to South America, but here was Quinn, about to carry her off to England without so much as a word.

'Let's go,' he snapped.

She looked up as he opened the door. The corduroy suit had clearly been his in the days before he'd matured. The jacket was too small; his shoulders seemed ready to burst the seams. He was wearing a blue turtleneck beneath the jacket, and it clung to him, clearly defining the ridged muscle in his chest and abdomen. Her glance fell lower, to the tightness of the corduroy trousers across his thighs and groin . . .

Something sharper than fear flared within her. 'I'm not going with you,' she said, taking a step back. 'You can't make me.' Quinn said nothing. He merely clasped her hand in his and tugged her out off the door. 'Damn you,' she hissed, 'you won't get away with this!'

He laughed softly. 'Get away with what, sweet Juliet? You make it sound as if I'm stealing you. You're with me of your own free will, remember? You can't live without me.' His voice grew cold and his fingers bit into hers. 'And neither can your father.'

His rental car was parked on the quiet street behind the Fowler house. The engine sounded as loud as a buzz-saw when he started it, and she looked towards the house, certain she'd see someone running towards them. But the house watched them with empty glass eyes, and soon they were moving swiftly along the silent suburban streets. When they reached the motorway, Quinn jammed his foot almost to the floor, and the car leaped ahead like a racehorse. He made only one step en route, at a service station along the road. Paige sat in the car, gripped by a strange lethargy, watching as he made a call from a telephone booth. His speech was animated, and she had the impression he was arguing with someone at the other end, but finally he laughed, slapped his hand against the side of the booth, and hung up. Less than half an hour later, they were on the east side of Manhattan, approaching Central Park.

Quinn slowed the car and pulled to the kerb in front of a handsome brownstone house. A man about his age stepped from the shadows, peered into the car, and smiled at Paige.

'No wonder you're in such a hurry, old man,' he said. 'All right, follow me.'

He climbed into a small Mercedes waiting at the kerb and pulled into the street. A dozen questions raced through Paige's mind, but she wasn't about to give Quinn the satisfaction of asking any of them. His silence would be hers, too. The cars wove through the streets of the city, from east side to west, through midtown traffic, until they reached lower Manhattan. At last, in an area given over to clusters of municipal buildings, Quinn's friend pulled to the kerb and parked. Quinn did the same.

'Get out,' he said to Paige.

They were the first words he'd spoken to her in hours. The man grinned at her as she stepped on to the pavement, and then he looked at Quinn.

'You're sure this is what you want, pal? No offence, sweetheart,' he added, flashing a smile at Paige. 'It's just that this is a mighty big step to take on the spur of the moment.'

That was when Paige's pulse began to race. 'Quinn?' she whispered, and he turned a cold, unsmiling face to her.

'Jim and I went to school together,' he said. 'And now he's the Mayor's number one boy.'

Paige's mouth went dry. 'Quinn,' she said again, and this time a mocking smile touched his mouth.

'Everything's all set—we can be married within the hour.' His eyes sought hers, and she drew in her breath when she saw their blue-green fire. 'Isn't that wonderful news, darling?'

'But . . . but I thought . . .'

Why was she so stunned? He'd told her he was going to marry her. In the last couple of hours, she'd even begun to believe it. But it couldn't happen so quickly, she thought, staring at him. Without realising it, she'd counted on time as her ally. There were laws and licences and blood tests . . .

Faintly, as if from a great distance, she heard Jim's puzzled laughter. 'Hey, pal, I thought you said the lady would be delighted.'

'She is,' Quinn said. His hand closed on the nape of her neck. 'She's just speechless. Aren't you, Paige?'

His voice was a smoky whisper as he drew her to him.

Paige's lashes fell to her cheeks. She wanted to hit out at him, to pound her fists against his chest—but a sweet weakness as heavy as cream was flooding through her.

'Don't,' she whispered, but it was meaningless. Quinn's mouth took hers and she swayed towards him, leaning into his encircling arm. She heard him make a soft sound in his throat, and then he pulled her so tightly against him that she felt her breasts flatten against his chest.

Jim laughed nervously. 'OK, guys. I'm convinced.'

When Quinn drew back and looked at her, his eyes were blue flames. 'Tell Jim you want to marry me,' he whispered.

Paige touched her tongue to her lips. 'I . . .'

'Tell him.'

She looked into his eyes. 'I want to marry Quinn,' she murmured.

She knew that both the question and answer were meant for Jim. But she thought she saw something ignite deep in the aquamarine depths of Quinn's eyes. Tears glistened on her lashes, and she blinked them away. When she looked into his eyes again, whatever she'd seen was gone, and she realised that all she'd seen was a reflection of her own anguish.

The tall building into which Quinn led her seemed empty at first. But there was a harried clerk waiting in an office that had clearly been opened for them and, in a tiled room, a lab attendant in a white coat greeted them with a sharp-needled syringe. Finally, in an apartment high above the East River, Paige and Quinn were married. A stranger in a dark suit asked the questions she'd expected to hear asked on this day, and she answered them. But the man who stood beside her wasn't Alan. It was Quinn who held her hand, Quinn who watched her face as she made her whispered replies, her hesitancy offset by his strong responses. He paused only when it came time to place the wedding ring on her finger.

There was no ring. Quinn looked over the judge's shoulder, to his friend, and Jim made a face and shrugged.

The judge marrying them cleared his throat. 'We can improvise,' he said. 'Do without, if necessary.'

But Quinn shook his head. 'Dammit,' he growled, 'there must be something we can use.'

There was. Paige drew in her breath and put her hand to her breast. 'Your ring,' she murmured.

Quinn misunderstood. 'I don't have it any more,' he said, and his mouth twisted strangely. 'I seem to have misplaced it.'

She felt the rush of colour to her cheeks as she reached beneath her suit jacket, into the scooped neckline of her silk blouse.

'You gave it to me,' she said in a thready whisper.

The ruby against her palm was like a burning ember as she held it out to him on its gold chain. He stared at for a long moment before slowly lifting his eyes to hers.

'You're wearing my ring.'

His voice had a quality that reminded her of grey summer skies on a northern lake. Paige nodded.

'Yes.'

The silence seemed to hang between them. Then, eyes still on Quinn's, she put her hands to her head and lifted her hair from her shoulders. She heard the sharp intake of his breath and then he reached behind her and unclasped the chain on which the ruby hung. His hand brushed her breasts as the ring tumbled into his palm, and his fingers closed tightly around it.

'Place the ring on Miss Gardiner's finger,' the judge said,

'and repeat after me. With this ring . . .'

Somehow, she managed to smile through the obligatory congratulations. Jim kissed her cheek, the judge shook her hand, and then, finally, she and Quinn were alone, speeding down the roadway to Kennedy Airport. Paige looked down at her hand, at the ruby that seemed to flame on her finger.

She was Quinn Fowler's wife, she thought dully. *His wife.*

She slipped the ring from her finger and held it out to him, as if the act would undo the vows he had forced her to take. His eyes moved swiftly from the road to her open palm and the blood-red stone.

'What am I supposed to do with that?' he asked.

'It's your ring. I thought you'd want it back.'

'Keep it,' he said gruffly. 'It has no meaning to me any more.'

Angry tears filled her eyes. God, how he hated her! She wanted to throw the ring at him—but something within her, nameless and only half glimpsed, stopped her. Her hands trembled as she looped the gold chain through the ring and hung it around her neck.

They said nothing more until they were settled in the first-class lounge at the airport. Quinn asked for a telephone and then turned to Paige.

'We have some calls to make,' he said. 'Can you manage to say the right things, or must I write a script for you?'

She looked at him. 'Calls? To whom?'

'To our families. Mine and yours. And Alan.'

His arrogance stunned her. 'Alan?' she repeated, her voice registering disbelief. 'But what will you say to him?'

Quinn's mouth curled in a tight smile. 'It's what he says to me that matters, Paige. Don't worry—I'll handle it.'

She gave him a cool look. 'I don't care if you handle it or not, Quinn. It's Alan I'm concerned about. He's bound to be hurting after what's happened.'

His eyebrows rose. 'It was going to happen anyway, Paige. The first story you gave me was that you weren't going ahead with the wedding.' His voice was soft, his sarcasm thinly veiled. 'Or was I mistaken?'

'But that's different. Changing my mind isn't the same as . . . as this.'

Quinn shrugged. 'I don't want Alan turning up on my doorstep,' he said roughly. 'I'd rather get everything settled now.'

She curled deeper into the leather couch, watching as he dialled, waiting for the explosion from the other end. But, when it came, it wasn't what she'd expected. She could tell, from Quinn's side of the conversation, that his parents were more upset by what their guests might have thought than by the emotional toll of the day's events on either of their sons. Quinn spoke to them politely but not defensively. He apologised for any embarrassment he might have caused them, explaining that what had happened between Paige and himself was inevitable. It was as if the subject under discussion involved a breach of etiquette, but nothing more than that.

When he asked to speak with Alan, Paige rose to her feet abruptly. But his hand caught hers and he pulled her back to sit beside him.

'Please,' she whispered, her face pale. 'I don't want to hear . . .'

His hand imprisoned hers, holding her by his side. Tears rose in her eyes as she listened to Quinn's explanation. His words were carefully chosen, surprisingly gentle, belying the pressure of his fingers on her wrist. She could see that it pained him to hurt his brother. After a long while, he nodded, and his eyes fastened on hers. The pressure on her wrist began to ease.

'Yes,' he said quietly, 'I'll tell her. I will, Alan. Of course I will. Thank you, Alan. Goodbye.'

She watched him while he hung up the phone. 'Quinn? Is Alan—is he all right?'

A muscle knotted in his jaw. 'He's fine.'

'Is he . . .' Her voice broke. 'Does he hate me very much?'

He looked at her, and a strange smile touched his mouth. 'No,' he said after a while, 'he doesn't hate you. He said—he said he wants us both to be happy.'

Paige's eyes filled with sudden tears. She hadn't loved Alan—but Alan had claimed to love her.

'He must have said more than that . . .'

Quinn reached out and brushed her tears away with his hand. 'What the hell did you expect him to say?' His voice was gruff, in strange contrast to the gentleness of his touch. 'What's the matter, Paige? Were you hoping he'd come after you?'

She shook her head. 'I only meant . . .'

'He told me to love you and take care of you. He . . .' His eyes raked hers, and she saw a darkness in the blue-green depths. 'He's hurt,' he said tersely, looking away from her. 'But it's better now than later.'

'All of this is my fault,' Paige sobbed. 'If only I . . .'

'If only you and your father hadn't got greedy,' Quinn said roughly. 'You have five minutes until we board. If you want to call your parents, do it now.'

Her hand shook as she dialled. But her mother was wonderful, laughing through her tears, reminding Paige that it had been she who'd advised her to follow her heart.

'Just be happy, dear,' she said, and Paige swallowed hard and assured her that she was.

Talking to her father was more difficult. She didn't know what to say, and the telephone line hummed in silence. Finally, without planning to say it, she whispered, 'Daddy?'

The word from her childhood surprised her.

'You caught us all off guard, Paige,' he said.

His voice held a false heartiness. She gripped the phone

more tightly and said again, 'Daddy? Quinn . . . Quinn knows. He knows everything.'

His breath whistled in her ear. 'Yes, all right,' he mumbled. 'Tell him—tell him it won't happen again. I'll make it right.'

It was such a raw admission of guilt that it rendered her speechless. She hung up the phone and looked at Quinn blankly.

'You—you were right about my father,' she whispered. 'He—he . . .'

The look on his face stunned her into silence. 'Stop it,' he growled, his face so close to hers that she felt his breath on her cheek. 'That act won't cut any ice, remember? You could have gone on fooling Alan until you'd wrung him dry, but I know the real you. Don't you ever forget it.'

A chill raced up her spine. She looked into Quinn's eyes and thought again of a predatory animal. His hand on her wrist, the look on his face, the possessiveness in the way he spoke—all were reminders of the fact that he held her captive.

'I won't forget anything,' she said bitterly. 'Believe me, Quinn, I'll remember everything you've done to me.'

He laughed as his eyes moved over her with slow insolence. 'You certainly will, sweet Juliet.'

There was no mistaking his meaning. She felt her cheeks flame with heat. Angry words crowded her throat, but she swallowed past them and turned from him in silence. She knew there was no sense answering him. He would only twist whatever she said and use it to his advantage. Her best defence—her only defence—was silence.

But keeping still became difficult as departure time neared. Quinn had volunteered no information about London, his home, or what he expected of her. Questions tumbled through her mind, but she asked none of them. She was sure that doing so would be a mistake; Quinn might see how frightened she really was—and she was determined never to give him that advantage.

In the narrow confines of the Concorde, the strange, empty darkness of the sky viewed through the window, the sense of being on a spaceship rather than a plane, underscored the surrealistic quality of the last few hours. She felt as if she were surrendering the life she'd known to the inky blackness of the night. She glanced at Quinn, silent and tight-lipped beside her, and she felt a sudden, swirling excitement.

What if things had gone differently? What if he really had fallen in love with her and asked her to run away with him? What if . . .

If, if, if. There was no point to playing that kind of game. And yet, Paige found herself stealing another look at the man beside her, remembering the things he'd whispered to her the night they'd met, the way he'd kissed her, the feel of his arms around her. If only time were a wheel, she thought suddenly, and you could turn it back. If only she'd met Quinn before she'd met Alan . . .

Quinn turned towards her and she looked away quickly. It wouldn't have mattered when they met. What she'd felt in Quinn's arms wasn't love. He would have asked her to go to bed with him, not to run away and marry him. That was the irony in all this, wasn't it? That he'd married her only because he believed she'd behaved like a tramp.

Her thoughts flashed nervously to what awaited her in London. She knew he owned a business there. Did he live in a hotel suite? He seemed the sort of man who might prefer that kind of impersonal setting. A furnished flat, perhaps. Yes, she thought, that was probably where he lived, and she let her mind drift, imagining some efficient but coldly decorated suite of rooms bearing no imprint of the man who lived in them.

London lay dark and silent when they landed. During the

taxi ride from the airport, Paige leaned her forehead against the window. *England,* she thought, waiting to feel something. But she was numb with weariness. The taxi finally pulled up before a grey stone house. Quinn stepped to the pavement and held his hand out to her.

'Your new home, Paige.' Cold amusement darkened his eyes. 'I hope it meets with your approval.'

She ignored his hand and moved past him, trying to think of some rejoinder that would mask the terror within her. But no words came, and her mouth went dry. She heard Quinn speak her name, and then his arms closed around her.

'I'm all right,' she murmured, but he'd already swung her into his arms.

'Like hell you are,' he growled, holding her close to him as he strode up the steps to the house.

The door swung open, and Quinn's housekeeper stared at them from the entranceway.

'Say "hello" to my wife, Norah,' he muttered as he marched past her.

The housekeeper bustled after them, wide-eyed with shock, offering coffee or tea, or something more celebratory, but Quinn headed straight for the curving staircase that rose to the next floor.

'Thank you, Norah, but Mrs Fowler's had a long day. I think what she needs most is sleep.'

Paige wanted to protest, to tell him she was capable of walking up the stairs on her own, but his arms were warm and strangely comforting. It was easier to clasp her hands around his neck and lay her face against his chest. By the time he shouldered open the door to a room at the end of the hall, her lashes lay heavy against her cheeks.

'That's it,' he said softly, and she felt herself sinking into the soft embrace of a wide bed.

There was the brush of his fingers at her throat, the

whisper of silk, and then her jacket was off her shoulders, her blouse unbuttoned to the cleft between her breasts. Quinn muttered something, and his fingers stilled. His hand lay unmoving on her breast.

Was it a dream, or did she hear her own voice whisper his name? Was there the brush of firm lips against hers? Was there a memory of heated skin? Did she hear a husky voice whisper, 'You'll be all right, Juliet?'

Yes, it was a dream. It had to be. The only reality, Paige thought as she fell into a dark spiral of exhaustion, was that Quinn had carried her off against her will.

He was her husband, and this was the England that had once known armoured knights and moated castles. But those days were long gone.

You might still be able to carry a woman off. Quinn had proved that. But you could never force her to belong to you. That would always remain the same.

CHAPTER SIX

DRESSED in her bridal gown, Paige walked slowly down a twisting corridor. Doors, closed against her for ever, watched her with blinded eyes. A man appeared far ahead. He was tall, broad-shouldered, and she moved towards him. He turned and made an impatient gesture. She began to walk more quickly, but it didn't seem to matter. The corridor grew ever longer, ever more twisted, until it was enclosed by high walls. The man was gone and Paige was alone in this strange place of shadows and darkness. Fear wrapped her in clammy embrace. Suddenly, there was a noise ahead, a tapping from behind the wall. Someone was there, someone who would help her . . .

'Mrs Fowler?'

Paige whimpered softly, still trapped in the tangled dream. There was a voice calling to her, but it was a strange voice.

The tapping came again. 'Mrs Fowler? Are you awake, ma'am? Mr Fowler said to tell you breakfast is ready.'

Mrs Fowler . . . Paige's eyes flew open. 'Alan?' she whispered.

The door swung open. A slender woman holding a silver tray stepped hesitantly into the darkened room.

'It's Norah, ma'am. I've brought you some coffee.' The woman put the tray on the bedside-table and then cleared her throat. 'Are you feeling better, Mrs Fowler? Shall I get you some aspirin or . . .'

'Norah?' Paige repeated, her voice still rough with sleep.

The woman nodded. 'The housekeeper, ma'am.' Her

eyes glinted with concern. 'Are you all right, Mrs Fowler?'

Paige moistened her lips with her tongue. 'Yes, I'm fine. I just . . .' Memory returned with a rush. *Mrs Fowler.* That was who she was. But she wasn't Alan's wife, she was Quinn's.

She sat up slowly and ran her hands through her hair. She felt light-headed, almost as if she'd had too much to drink. It was jet-lag, she thought, the result of concentrating yesterday afternoon and evening into a four-hour flight on the Concorde from New York. And it was something more, it was the way her life had changed in the last hours.

Norah was saying something about it being a lovely day. Paige looked up and smiled tentatively.

'I'm sorry, Norah. I seem to be a bit foggy. What time did you say it was?'

'Just past eight, ma'am.'

Paige put her hands to her head. 'Morning or evening?' she asked with a little laugh.

Norah smiled. 'Morning, ma'am. Woud you like me to run a bath for you?'

'No, thank you.'

The woman nodded. 'I've set breakfast in the library. I hope that meets with your approval.'

After all that had happened to her, the thought that anyone should even wonder about her approval made Paige laugh. The housekeeper's brows rose.

'Are you sure you're all right, Mrs Fowler? Perhaps I should send Mr Fowler to you.'

'No,' Paige said sharply, and then she took a breath. 'No, thank you, Norah,' she said carefully. 'I'm fine.' She smiled as she tossed back the covers. 'A cup of coffee is . . .'

Her words tumbled to a halt as she glanced down at herself. She was dressed in a nightgown, one of the lace ones her mother had bought for her trousseau. But when . . . ? And who . . . ? She had a swift, heart-stopping memory of strong, tanned hands brushing against her skin, undoing the buttons of her blouse. But there was nothing after that image.

'Ma'am?'

Paige drew a breath. 'Just tell my—tell Mr Fowler I'll be down in a few minutes. I'm just going to unpack.'

The housekeeper shook her head. 'I'll do that while you're at breakfast, ma'am. I'd have done it last night, after Mr Fowler sent me upstairs to help you into your nightgown. But he said not to disturb you, so . . .'

Paige laughed shakily. 'You mean you . . . Thanks, Norah. I'm not usually so helpless.'

The woman smiled pleasantly. 'You weren't helpless at all, Mrs Fowler. You were just exhausted. And who wouldn't be, after such an exciting day? It's so romantic.'

Paige, who had swung her legs to the floor and was pouring a cup of coffee, glanced up.

'Romantic?'

'Your elopement, ma'am. Who would have thought Mr Fowler would come home with a bride?'

A flush swept across Paige's cheeks. 'Indeed,' she said, forcing a smile through stiff lips, 'who would have thought?'

The artificial smile fell from her face as the door closed. Exciting, she thought bitterly. Romantic. Oh, yes, that was what everyone thought. No one dreamed that she'd come to this London house unwillingly, more a captive than a bride. Quinn had arranged for the world to see them as lovers, caught in a passion beyond their control, and he'd done a damned good job. The Fowlers believed it, her parents believed it—and Alan believed it. Only she and Quinn knew the ugly truth.

Paige put down her cup and walked to the window. Heavy curtains covered it, and she drew them aside and looked out into the sunlit street. London, she thought, watching the unfamiliar scene below. The house was on a quiet mews—Mayfair, Quinn had told the taxi driver who'd brought them from the airport. Under other circumstances, she would have been dancing with excitement, delighted by the charm of the cobblestone street, the narrow Edwardian houses, and the cars that drove on the wrong side of the road.

She let the curtain fall into place again. The street below only emphasised her feeling of displacement. She was in a strange country and she knew no one. There was only Quinn. It was as if the clock had been turned back four or five centuries and he had ridden in on a prancing stallion and stolen her away. She was his hostage.

Paige drew a deep breath as she began to dress. It was time to face Quinn and set the rules for her new life. There would be 'compensations', he'd said, a million years ago when he'd taken her from the Fowler house. She hadn't answered him them; she'd been too stunned by everything that was happening. But she would answer him now. She would tell him that there were limits to what he could demand of her. She might be his prisoner, but she would never be his slave.

The hall outside her room was silent. She'd seen little of the house the night before. From the shelter of Quinn's arms, she'd only glimpsed dark walls and shadowed corners. Now, daylight revealed a handsome, eclectically furnished home that bore a clear masculine imprint. No moats or drawbridges here, she thought with a nervous laugh as she started down the stairs.

The house was clearly Quinn's. There were framed photographs on the walls, black and white studies of city streets and country lanes, all with the same quality of moodiness flowing like dark rivers just beneath. Paige knew immediately that Quinn had taken them. A stack of letters lay on a table in the entry hall, all addressed in the firm, flowing script she recognised as his. A tweed jacket lay draped carelessly over the back of a chair. His, she thought, touching her hand to it, and she felt the sudden, heavy thud of her heart.

Music drifted towards her from a door that stood ajar just down the hall. Mozart, she thought, walking slowly towards it. At the doorway, she paused, her mouth suddenly dry. Alone in the guest-room, it had been easy to tell herself she would lay down the rules that would govern her new life. Now, with the moment at hand, she knew it wouldn't be half as simple as she'd let herself think. But she would do it—that was what counted. Determination squared her shoulders, and she took a step forward and rapped on the partly open door.

'Come in, Paige. Close the door behind you.'

Quinn was seated at an old-fashioned partners' desk on the far side of the room. As she entered, he rose and dropped a handful of papers on the desk's cluttered surface.

The room was pleasant. A brass and teak wood campaign table stood near the desk, topped by a sleek computer. The walls were lined with books and more photographs, some of them unframed and simply tacked in place. The room's focal point was a handsome marble fireplace; coals glowed in the heart, chasing the morning's chill. Net-curtained french doors overlooked what she assumed was a garden, and a table set for two stood before them.

Her eyes returned to Quinn. He was wearing pale grey trousers and a blue sweater, and he was watching her with a bemused expression.

'What do you think?' he asked. 'Do you like the room?'

Paige looked at him steadily. 'Norah said you wanted to see me.'

His eyebrows rose. 'That wasn't precisely the message I sent. I asked her to tell you breakfast was ready.'

A light flush brushed her cheeks. 'Yes, that's what she

said. But I never have breakfast, thank you. I only take coffee in the morning. And . . .'

'Nor do I,' he said pleasantly. 'But I thought, since this was such a special day . . .'

Her flush deepened, and she started to turn away, determined not to be drawn into a game of cat and mouse. 'If that's all you wanted . . .'

'Do you like your coffee black? Or with cream and sugar?' He crossed the room to the neatly set table and looked at her.

'Black. But . . .'

'Black,' he repeated, picking up a silver coffee-pot. An aromatic fragrance filled the room as he filled two cups and held one out to her. 'I'll remember that. A husband should know how his wife likes her coffee, don't you think?'

Now, she thought, and she took a breath.

'Quinn, there are things we should discuss . . .'

'Coffee first,' he said. 'After that, I'll consider a discussion.' He sipped at his coffee and then looked at her again. 'Are you feeling better?'

She nodded. 'Much. I . . . I was just tired, I guess. I . . .'

A slow smile curled at the corners of his mouth. 'Yes, I know. When I looked in on you . . .'

She drew in her breath. 'When you . . . when you looked in on me?'

'Yes. You were dead to the world.'

The dream-image came again. *Heated skin against hers, lips brushing hers with the lightest of kisses . . .*

'And then, when I saw you this morning, I was tempted to let you sleep as long as you liked. But that only makes the time change more difficult.' Quinn cocked his head to the side. 'Is something wrong with your coffee, Paige?'

But he knew what was wrong, damn him. She could see the amusement in the cold, ocean-blue depths of his eyes.

'You were in my room during the night and again this morning?' He shook his head. 'But you said . . .'

'I was in *my* room,' he said softly.

His room. She had slept in his room. In his bed.

'Your room.' Spoken aloud, the words seemed to tremble in the air. 'I thought . . . I assumed I was in the guest-room.'

Quinn's eyes met hers. 'Why would my wife sleep in the guest-room?'

'Quinn . . .'

He smiled. '*I* slept in the guest-room, Paige.'

Air rushed from her lungs. 'That wasn't necessary.' The blush tinged her skin again. 'I mean, I'll take the guest-room. I don't mind . . .'

'But I do.' His voice was flat, the words sharp.

'Really, Quinn, it'll be fine. I . . .'

'I don't think you understand me, Paige. We're not sleeping in separate rooms.'

'I have no intention of . . .' Her voice faltered.

'You're my wife,' he said, as if that were the only explanation required. His eyes moved over her slowly; she could almost feel their caress. 'Norah thought it was gallant of me to let you catch up on your sleep our first night together.'

'I don't give a damn what Norah thought. I . . .'

'The truth wasn't half as respectable.' His words cut across her like lightning through the night sky. 'I want you wide awake and ready when we make love, Paige.' His eyes caught hers. 'That's why I stayed out of our bed last night.'

Our bed. She stared at him, wondering if he could hear the pounding of her heart, telling herself he'd chosen such blunt words deliberately to put her off balance. But one look at his face, at the defiant set of his jaw and the fierce glow in his eyes, told her that what he'd said had been the naked truth.

Paige marched across the room and put her cup and saucer on the table. 'That's out of the question,' she said quickly. 'We're not . . .'

'We're not what? Not husband and wife?' He laughed. 'There's a very official-looking document on my desk that says we are.'

'Our marriage is a sham,' she said, lifting her chin defiantly. 'We both know it, Quinn. We . . .'

He was across the room in a few quick strides, looming over her as she shrank back against the wall.

'Listen to me, sweet Juliet,' he said softly. 'I love my brother, but I'm not a candidate for sainthood. Marrying you to protect Alan was one thing, but getting no benefit from the arrangement is quite another.' She pulled her head away as he reached toward her, but he caught her chin in his hand and turned her face to him. 'I'll be damned if I'm going to come out of this the only loser.'

She forced her eyes to meet his without flinching. 'What have you lost, Quinn?' she asked softly. 'You hurt your brother, embarrassed your family, ruined my life . . .'

His hand tightened as it slid to the nape of her neck. 'Ruined your life?' His voice was as quiet as as a graveyard. 'You came out ahead, my love. You wanted to marry money—I have money, Paige, more than Alan could have given you. You wanted to marry a Fowler—hell, you had to marry one, for Daddy's sake. Well, I'm a Fowler.' His lips drew back from his teeth. 'Not the one you'd planned on—but that's an advantage, isn't it?'

'Don't compare yourself to Alan,' Paige said quickly. 'You're nothing like him.'

She drew in her breath as Quinn pulled her to him. 'Exactly,' he said in a low whisper. 'Just think of how much more you'll enjoy being in my bed than in his.'

She felt the blood drain from her face. 'That's disgusting!

You . . .'

'Now I can see it,' Quinn said softly. 'That innocent tremor in your lips, that look of fear in your eyes . . .' His thumb moved lightly along the column of her throat. 'No wonder Alan thought . . .'

'I won't sleep with you,' she said sharply.

'You'll do what our contract calls for.'

'Our what?'

'Our contract. Our marriage vows.' He smiled coldly. 'Don't tell me you've forgotten our arrangement already.'

Paige touched the tip of her tongue to her lips. 'That's exactly what it was. An arrangement. And . . .'

'I know the terms, Paige. Believe me, I have no illusions about a grand passion.'

'Neither do I. And that's why . . .'

'You would have preferred Alan, wouldn't you?' His voice rose. 'He'd have been so much easier to handle. He'd have never demanded anything, never questioned anything—and he'd have been grateful for any crumbs you tossed him.' His hands closed on her shoulders. 'But I'm not Alan.'

Tears gathered at the corners of her eyes. 'No,' she said quickly. 'You're nothing like Alan. He's kind and considerate, and . . .'

'And he's no match for a bitch like you.'

She twisted against the steely strength of his hands. 'Don't call me that, damn you. I . . .'

'Come on, Paige, don't give me that nonsense. We both know what you are.'

'You don't know anything about me,' she whispered.

'I know everything about you. It's only Alan who doesn't. You came on to me like . . .'

'That didn't bother you when you thought I was engaged to someone else, did it?' she asked defiantly. ' "The hell with your fiancé", you said. "Forget him," you said.

But when you realised I was engaged to Alan . . .'

'When I realised you'd deceived him into thinking you were something you weren't, you mean.' A muscle moved in his jaw. 'I know how to deal with a woman like you,' he said softly. 'Alan doesn't. The innocent need someone to protect them. That's why I had to take you from him.'

Paige looked into his face. 'Very touching,' she said. 'Quinn makes a sacrifice for his little brother.'

'Meaning?'

She smiled coldly. 'Is that the reason you'd like to believe?'

His eyes grew dark. 'What the hell kind of question is that?'

'Just listen to yourself, Quinn,' she said in a venom-filled voice. 'All that talk about "protecting" the innocent. Is blackmailing women into your bed part of the "protection" you so generously offer?'

'Damn you, Paige . . .'

'Why don't you try being honest with yourself? You didn't marry me to protect Alan. You did it because you wanted me for yourself.'

His hands dug into her as he drew her to him. 'You'd love to believe that, wouldn't you?'

'I don't know why I didn't see it before,' she said, reckless with the desire to hurt him. 'Were you trying to fool me or yourself? Not that it matters—we both know the truth, don't we? I'll bet you used to take Alan's toys away from him, too.'

He laughed at her. 'I'm almost nine years older than Alan, Paige. The only things I've ever taken from him were things that would hurt him.' He paused, and a smile that was no smile turned the corner of his mouth. 'Like you, for instance.'

'What do you know about me or Alan? You've been out of his life for years, playing at living abroad, toying with computers . . .'

His eyes narrowed as he looked at her. 'I hate to disappoint you, but that's not quite the way it was. I haven't "played" at anything. I've had to work damned hard for what I've got.'

'It's Alan who's worked hard, shouldering the whole burden at Fowler's after you walked out.'

His hands fell from her shoulders. 'You don't know a damned thing about it,' he said softly.

Watching his face, she knew she'd somehow cut through the cool surface and touched some hidden vulnerability. She spoke quickly, searching for words that might wound him.

'I know enough. You left your family . . .'

'I sure as hell did.' He laughed at her expression of distaste. 'I left by request—didn't Alan tell you?'

Paige stared at him. 'You mean, your parents asked you to leave?'

He smiled. 'I couldn't have phrased it better myself.'

So much for wounding him. 'You sound—you sound proud of it.'

'Damned right, I'm proud. What I've done . . .'

'Poor Alan. "My big brother", he calls you. And he talks about you as if . . . as if you were special.' She looked at him and then turned her face away. 'I'm glad he doesn't know the truth.'

'Such devotion,' Quinn said softly.

Paige's eyes blazed with anger. 'I know it's beyond you to understand, but I don't want to see Alan hurt.'

He dipped his head in mock appreciation. 'Nice. If I didn't know you better, I'd be tempted to believe it.'

'If only you'd never come back,' she hissed. 'If only you'd stayed away.'

'But I didn't stay away,' he said, swinging her towards him. 'The prodigal son returned—and ruined all your pretty little plans. Hard luck, sweetheart.'

'It's useless to argue with you, isn't it? You're so damned sure you're right . . .'

'I'm right about you, Paige. I know you'll find it difficult to believe, but women like you aren't unique.'

She looked up at him. 'What's that supposed to mean?'

'Just what it says. I've met your type before. Women like you sell yourselves for whatever you can get. Quick sex or a long tease—whatever the occasion or the purchaser requires —you can manage either one.'

'God, how I loathe you! No wonder your parents tossed you out. You were probably the sort of little boy who pulled wings off flies.'

He laughed. 'I was the sort who thought for myself, Paige. I still do. If Alan had ever developed the ability, he'd have seen right through your Snow Queen act.'

Her face whitened. 'You have no right to say that to me,' she whispered. 'I never lied to Alan about . . . about that. He knew . . .'

'He didn't know a damned thing. You had the poor bastard half convinced you were Sleeping Beauty and he was the Prince whose kiss would awaken you.' He clasped her shoulders tightly and drew her to him. 'If only he knew the truth.'

'I never led your brother on,' Paige said, trying to twist free to him. 'He was the one who pursued me. I . . .'

'Yeah, I'll bet he did,' he said, his voice sharp with sarcasm. 'You worked him like a trained donkey. Dangle the carrot and he'd follow you anywhere. And it would have worked—if you hadn't run into me.'

Paige lifted her chin. 'Back to square one. "Quinn saves Alan from the clutches of *la femme fatale*." I'm surprised you didn't tell your whole family about me—if they'd believed your lies, you'd have been transformed from black sheep to hero overnight.' Her eyes flashed defiance.

'I hope you're not crazy enough to think what you've done is your ticket back, Quinn. Your name's blacker than ever now.'

He laughed, a soft, frightening sound, and mimed applause. 'Fantastic performance. I take back what I said before, Paige. Your trade isn't unique, but your talents may be. A little amateur psychology, a little method acting—damn, but you're good.' His hands slid to her waist and he pulled her against him. 'But not good enough.'

Fear shot through her as she felt the heat of his body against hers.

'Let go of me,' she said carefully.

He smiled coldly. 'Did that work with Alan?' She gasped as he moved against her, letting her feel his power. 'Because it sure as hell doesn't mean a damned thing to me.'

'Don't . . .'

His hands slid up her back and he cupped her face, tilting it up to his. 'That's not what you said on the beach.'

'I should have,' she said quickly. 'And I'm saying it now. Please . . .'

'The return of the Snow Queen,' he said softly. 'How charming.' His thumbs moved slowly along her throat, and he gave her a quick, dangerous smile. 'But it's too late to try that, Paige. It won't play, not with me.'

'Can't you . . . can't you forget that night?' she asked desperately. 'I've told you and told you, it was a mistake. It was . . .'

His hands curved around her neck. 'I've known many women, sweet Juliet.' His voice was soft, his eyes dark. 'Some of them wanted to play games that might even make *you* blush. But what happened on that beach . . .'

Her hands spread on his chest. 'I . . . I don't want to talk about it. It was . . . it was as if . . .'

He laughed softly. 'You don't have to tell me what it was like. I remember—I'll always remember.' His voice hardened. 'Why didn't you come back to me?'

'I . . . I couldn't. People were . . . people were waiting. And . . . and it seemed wrong. I was . . . I was marrying Alan in just a few days. I was . . .'

His eyes darkened. 'You were afraid of getting caught.'

'Yes. No, no, it wasn't like that. I . . . I was confused. I didn't want to hurt Alan. I . . .'

'You mean, you didn't want to lose the pay-off you'd worked so hard to collect. You went back into that ballroom and you panicked. What if someone had seen us? All your plans, up in smoke.'

'You're wrong, Quinn. I . . .'

She tried to turn her face away from him, but his hands held her immobilised.

'No sex without marriage. That's it, isn't it? That was how you snared Alan in the first place.'

'I've had enough. I won't let you say these things to me. I . . .'

'But you'd have slept with him after the wedding.' A terrible weariness was stealing into her bones, sapping her of strength. 'Answer me,' he growled. 'Would you have let him make love to you?'

'Yes,' she murmured.

'Because he was your husband.'

'Yes,' she said again.

Quinn inhaled sharply. 'Because that would have been his payment for making you a Fowler.'

Her head rose sharply. 'No. Damn you, Quinn . . .'

Something evil stirred in the darkness of his eyes. 'Well,' he said softly, 'you're a Fowler now, Paige.' His hands slid down her throat, to her shoulders, down her spine. She moaned as he cupped her buttocks and drew her against him. 'And it's payment time.'

She began to tremble in his arms. 'Don't do this, Quinn. We made a deal . . .'

'Yes. I said I'd protect your father if you married me.'

'And I married you, Quinn. I . . .'

His hands moved on her body, slowly kindling a heat deep within her. 'Yes,' he whispered. 'You did. And now I want you in my bed.'

His touch was sure and knowing, and she began to tremble beneath it.

'Let me go home, Quinn,' she breathed. 'I beg you . . .'

'This *is* your home, Paige.'

'Give me a divorce. An annulment . . .'

He laughed softly. 'There won't be any grounds for annulment—not after tonight.'

With her last bit of effort, Paige raised her head and looked into his eyes.

'I hope you burn in hell,' she said.

A light flickered and died in the sea-dark depths of his eyes.

'Sometimes, sweet Juliet,' he whispered, 'I think I already am.'

CHAPTER SEVEN

'MRS FOWLER? May I come in, ma'am?'

Paige turned from the mirror. 'Yes, Norah. What is it?'

The door swung open and the housekeeper stepped into the room. 'I thought I'd stop in before . . .' She paused and put her hand to her mouth. 'Don't you look lovely in that dress, Mrs Fowler? Such a perfect colour for you.'

Paige glanced into the mirror again. The gown Quinn had bought her that afternoon was made of velvet. It *was* lovely, she thought—or it would have been, under other circumstances.

'Yes,' she said with a careless shrug, 'I suppose it is.'

Norah touched a silk chemise that lay draped across the chair. 'Everything's so beautiful,' she said, smiling at Paige. 'Are you sure you don't want me to empty the rest of those boxes?'

Paige looked across the room at the stack of unopened boxes that still lay beside the wardrobe. 'No, thank you, Norah. I'll take care of it later.'

'Oh, but I don't know if you'll have time.' Norah's face reddened. 'I mean, Mr Fowler's planned a lovely evening. He asked me to set the table in the library, and to chill some champagne.'

'That's all right,' Paige said quickly. 'I'll . . . I'll find the time Was there anything else, Norah?'

The housekeeper shook her head. 'I just wanted to let you know that I was off, ma'am.' She put her hand on the doorknob and smiled at Paige. 'I called my sister and told her I was coming for a surprise visit. She was delighted

—and I told her about all the lovely things you gave me for my niece. I can't thank you enough, Mrs Fowler. Such nice dresses and all—and new, most of them. Lila will be so pleased.'

'Yes, I hope she is, Norah. If that's all . . .'

The housekeeper tapped her finger against her mouth. 'I think so,' she mused. 'The duck is in the chafing dish, and the bisque is ready. Mr Fowler said not to worry, that he'll take care of things.'

Paige turned away quickly. 'Yes,' she said, 'I'm sure he will.'

'Well, I'll be on my way, then.' She paused at the door. 'You're sure about the clothing, are you, ma'am? I couldn't believe it when Mr Fowler said to toss it all away. I . . .'

Paige patted the woman's arm. 'I'm glad your niece can make use of it,' she said quickly. 'Tell her . . . tell her to enjoy everything.'

The woman smiled again as she pulled open the door. 'Isn't he something?' Paige looked at her questioningly. 'Mr Fowler, ma'am. Why on earth would he want you to throw away such a lovely trousseau?'

Because he's a bastard . . . 'I . . . I'm sure I don't know, Norah.'

'Well, goodnight, ma'am.'

'Goodnight, Norah.'

Paige managed to keep smiling until the door swung shut, and then she sank down on the bed and glanced at the clock. Almost eight. Almost zero hour, she thought bitterly. Quinn had, indeed, taken care of things. Chilled champagne, the clinging, velvet dress she wore that he had selected and bought—he'd even thought of giving Norah the night off. Was he afraid Paige would cry out for help when he . . . when he took her to his bedroom?

She rose and paced across the room. He needn't have worried, she thought grimly. She had no intention of giving him the satisfaction of any kind of response, not even a negative one. She would do what was demanded of her, just as she had all day, starting this morning when he'd calmly told her she was to dispose of her trousseau. Everything he'd done—and would do tonight—was meant to remind her that he owned her. She bore his name, she lived in his house. She was his.

Paige glanced at her reflection. Her face was pale, except for two spots of colour high on her cheekbones. She touched her damp palms to her face. *Don't let Quinn see how frightened you are.* He had all the advantages as it was. As for passion—it was hard to remember she'd ever felt any for him. Being seduced was one thing; a command performance was quite another, and that's what this was, after all. 'Payment time,' he'd said that morning. And the time was now.

Champagne. And candles, probably. Soft music. Quinn wasn't a barbarian—if he could seduce her, he would. And if he couldn't . . . A shudder ran through her. Nothing would stop him. He was a man who knew what he wanted and got it. Always. He'd spent the day proving that to her.

'Where do you think you're going?' His voice had cracked after her like a whip as she'd hurried from the library that morning.

'To my room,' she'd said defiantly.

She'd waited, half expecting him to remind her that she had no room to call her own, but he only shook his head.

'We're going out. Get your coat.'

'Out? But . . .'

'Get your coat,' he'd repeated impatiently. 'We have a great deal to do.'

In the car, he told her that she was to dispose of everything she'd brought with her.

'Give it to Norah, if you like. She has a niece or a

cousin or something . . .'

'But . . . but all my things are new, Quinn. It doesn't make any sense.'

The face he turned towards her was cold. 'I've already told Norah she may take what she wishes. She said to tell you she was very grateful.'

Paige's mouth trembled. 'I'm sure she was,' she said stiffly, and then she turned away and stared blindly out the window of the dark green Jaguar.

He'd given away her things without even consulting her. She had no difficulty figuring out the reasons—he was separating her from her former life and, at the same time, branding her as his possession. And she was helpless against him. The streets rolled by, colours blending one into the other as they took in the sights. Buckingham Palace, and the black busbys and red coats of the Grenadier Guards; Whitehall, and the black and silver of a Guard mounted on a horse so still it might have been carved of granite; the Union Jack, flapping red, white, and blue above the Houses of Parliament.

How could the day be so beautiful and her heart so filled with sorrow?

And yet, there had been quick flashes of something else. There had been the old man marching through Piccadilly Circus, back stiff, eyes straight ahead, carrying a sign that explained that a diet high in protein was the cause of all the sin in the world. It had seemed natural to laugh and turn to Quinn beside her, saying—before she could think—that surely the old man had a double in New York who put blame on the meat-eaters. Quinn had laughed, too, until their eyes had met, and then their laugher had died.

And there had been that moment when they had stood in a little boutique off Bond Street, Paige trying on the velvet dress she wore now. The sales clerk had bubbled with delight as Quinn pointed an imperious finger at half a dozen outfits among those she'd shown them.

'We'll take those,' he said.

'And the dress Madam's wearing?' the clerk had asked. 'It's so perfect for her—that lavender's the very colour of her eyes.'

'No,' Quinn said quickly, 'no, it isn't. Her eyes are darker—the colour of violets.'

Paige's heart stopped as she looked at him in the mirror. For a flash of eternity, they were alone, on a windswept beach. And then the clerk giggled knowingly. Quinn's eyes narrowed and he let out his breath.

'We'll take the dress, too,' he'd said roughly, and the fragile moment was gone for ever.

They had never recaptured it, not in any of the shops or boutiques, not in the urbane bustle of Harrods. In each, Quinn had pointed to whatever struck his fancy, and Paige had listlessly tried on a seemingly endless array of woollens and silks and cashmeres, dresses and skirts, sweaters and trousers, and all of it might as well have been made of sackcloth.

'Tell me what you like,' Quinn said.

Her answer was always the same. 'It doesn't matter.'

After a while, his answer became as predictable as hers. 'We'll take it all,' he would say gruffly, and eventually the boxes stacked in the boot and back seat of the Jaguar overflowed and Quinn had to tell the wide-eyed sales clerks to arrange for delivery of the things he'd bought with such careless abandon.

The last thing he bought her was a wedding ring. Jewels gleamed against black velvet everywhere in the hushed shop to which he took her.

The jeweller seated them, then brought out trays of magnificent rings, all burning with the fires of diamonds, emeralds, and sapphires.

Quinn's eyes were expressionless as Paige stared at the

gleaming display. 'Pick whatever you like,' he said, dismissing them with a glance.

A band set with rubies winked up at her, and she thought of the blood-red stone that lay between her breasts, hidden from the world beneath her blouse, and of the night Quinn had given it to her. A lump rose to her throat.

'I don't want any of these,' she said to the jeweller. 'Haven't you something plain?'

The jeweller shrugged. 'If madam really prefers . . .'

'Have you something or not?' Quinn snapped.

'Yes, of course. But these . . .'

'Get my wife what she asked for.'

When they stood outside the shop again, Quinn looked at her, a strangely guarded expression on his face.

'Are you sure that's the ring you want?'

Paige looked at the narrow gold band on her finger and nodded. 'Yes. You've . . . you've bought me too much as it is.'

He put his hand on her arm. 'You're my wife,' he answered, as if that explained everything.

Her eyes closed briefly. 'I know what I am,' she whispered. 'You don't have to dress me in your colours just to remind me.'

'Is that what you think I'm doing?'

'Why else would you do it?' she said with a bitterness that surprised her, and before he could answer she pulled free of his hand and stepped off the kerb.

Everything happened at once. A horn blared, almost in her ear, Quinn's arm closed around her and lifted her on to the pavement beside him, and a blur of red shot by—a bus, Paige saw with horror—moving swiftly over the place in the road where she'd just been standing.

'You little fool!' Quinn snarled, spinning her towards him. 'You almost got yourself killed.'

'I . . . I forgot about the traffic,' she said breathlessly.

'I . . .'

Inexplicably, her eyes had filled with tears. 'What is it?' he demanded. 'Paige . . .'

She looked up at him. His eyes were fierce, protective. *You're my wife.* Her pulse tripped and she swayed against him.

His hands bit into her. 'Let's go home,' he said thickly.

Reality returned with a rush. 'You'll get what you paid for tonight, Quinn. Can't you wait another few hours?'

Lines cut into the skin beside his mouth. 'Paige . . .'

'And that house isn't my home. It never will be.'

His mouth hardened. 'Damned right it isn't,' he growled. Her heels clattered against the pavement as he tugged her towards his car. 'I'll see to that.'

They were silent as he raced the car through the London streets, charging forward at light changes and sliding through traffic with reckless abandon. By the time he pulled to a stop before a brick house on a quiet street, they were as remote from each other as they'd been during the flight on the Concorde.

'I've asked my solicitor to draw up some papers,' Quinn said in clipped tones. 'This won't take long.'

Quinn's solicitor was polite, but obviously uncomfortable.

'We do this all the time, Mrs Fowler,' he said, shoving a long, legal document across his desk.

'What is this?' she asked, but it was Quinn who answered.

'A nuptial contract. In the event I should divorce you, you're entitled to your clothing and ten thousand pounds.' His eyes raked her face. 'Fair enough, all things considered. Don't you agree, Paige?'

Her eyes had met his without flinching. 'And if I divorce you?'

Quinn had smiled. 'You won't,' he'd said softly. 'Or have you forgotten your father?'

The sight of his solicitor's pale, disbelieving face had given her the courage she needed, 'I won't sign this,' she'd said, shoving the papers aside.

Quinn had laughed aloud. 'Now we get down to basics, hmm?'

Her smile had been cool. 'Absolute basics. All I want from you is the price of a one-way plane ticket to the States.'

The solicitor had cleared his throat. 'Really, Mrs Fowler, that's most irregular.'

Her husband's smile had been as cool as hers. 'What's the game this time, darling?' he'd asked softly.

Paige had lifted her chin. 'What does it matter? As long as you're the winner.'

'Done,' he'd said.

Now, looking into the mirror, the velvet dress Quinn had bought her soft on her shoulders, Paige realised that he owned her, and he could discard her at will. And he would. The agreement she'd signed with such bravado convinced her of it. When he was tired of her, when he'd had enough of venting his anger on her body, he would send her away. Passion had nothing to do with why he wanted her. Not that it mattered: anger, desire, passion—it turned out they all led to the same end.

The clock chimed eight. Zero hour. Time for the dinner performance. Her hand reached to the light switch and she plunged the room into darkness.

Alan had tried to tell her that sex had nothing to do with love or happiness. It was just too bad she hadn't believed him.

Quinn was waiting for her in the library, as he had been that morning. She paused, watching him from the doorway. The table by the french doors was formally set, complete with flowers, Paige noted with a touch of bitterness. There were two fluted glasses and a wine-bucket on

Quinn's desk. The lights were low, and yes, as she'd expected, there was music—a Rachmaninov concerto, playing softly in the background. The perfect seduction scene, she told herself . . . and then Quinn rose to his feet and turned to face her.

Her heart rose to her throat. How could she hate him and still feel this way when she saw him? He was dressed as he'd been when they'd met, in a dinner-suit and ruffled shirt. His eyes blazed as they swept over her. *He was so beautiful . . . like a lion in his prime.*

A quick smile tilted at his mouth. 'Good evening,' he said softly.

'Good evening.' She looked at him again, her eyes lingering on his, and she flushed. 'I'm sorry I took so long, but . . .'

'It was worth the waiting. You look beautiful, Paige.'

The flush deepened. 'Thank you. But it's not me, it's this dress you bought.'

'Would you like some champagne?'

'No. I mean, yes, thank you, I would.'

Champagne would make what would happen next easier, she thought, watching as he opened the bottle with expert ease. Wasn't wine supposed to make you giddy and dull your senses? She took the glass he held out to her, smiling stiffly.

'Norah's left us quite a feast. It's all waiting for us. Whenever you're ready . . .'

'Whenever you're ready. 'Not yet,' she said quickly. Too quickly. Quinn looked at her, one eyebrow raised appraisingly. 'I . . . I'd like some more champagne first,' she said, tilting the glass to her lips and draining the pale gold liquid. 'It's very good.'

He smiled as he refilled her glass. 'You're supposed to sip it,' he said.

'Does it matter? Just so long as . . .'

His face darkened. 'Ah,' he said softly, 'now I understand. Just so long as you get drunk, hmm?'

'Look, Quinn . . . what do you think you're doing?'

'Taking the champagne from you. I don't want you sick to your stomach, Paige. We'll have dinner, and . . .'

'No, of course you don't want me sick,' she said bitterly. 'Not tonight.'

Quinn's arm slid lightly around her waist. 'Not any night,' he said mildly, as he led her to the table. 'The last time I helped someone who was drunk. I didn't do much of a job of it.'

'The mighty Quinn Fowler, not good at something?' Paige laughed sharply as he served her. 'I can hardly believe my ears. Whoever told you that much have been lying.'

He smiled. 'Alan's the one who said it. It was years ago, just before I left home. We were both—well, let's say we weren't feeling any pain. Alan was twelve, and he'd drunk the the best part of a six-pack . . .' He shook his head at the memory. 'Damn, but he was plastered.'

Paige's eyes flashed indignation. 'No wonder your parents tossed you out,' she said. 'Getting a twelve-year-old boy drunk on beer, and then laughing about it . . .'

'Sorry, but I can't take credit for it. Little brother got bombed all on his own. he was out with some buddies of his, and he came sneaking in just after I got back from a friend's wedding.' He glanced at her. 'Didn't he ever tell you this story?'

Paige shook her head. 'No,' she said slowly, thinking of how little Alan and she had ever really shared with each other. 'No, he didn't.'

Quinn nodded. 'Probably too embarrassed,' he said with a smile. 'Not that it was so awful—he was just a kid, experimenting, wanting to be an adult before he knew that adults just want to be kids. We shared a bathroom and—

well, let's just say I heard him being ill. Of course, I went to help him.' He grinned at the memory. 'Trouble was, my stomach wasn't any too solid at that moment. So when I saw what was happening to Alan . . .' He laughed and shook his head. 'When my mother found us, she was furious.'

It was hard not to smile. 'Yes, I can imagine. What did she do? Send you both to your rooms?'

Quinn's smile faded. 'That's what she did with Alan. As for me—I was a little too old to be sent to my room.' He lay down his knife and fork and pushed back his chair. 'So my old man did the next best thing. He told me to leave.'

Paige looked at him blankly. 'Leave? But you hadn't done anything.'

'That depends on your point of view. I can't believe Alan didn't tell you any of this. It was pretty upsetting to him.'

'We . . . Alan and I didn't . . .' Paige looked up from her plate. 'You and he really were close, weren't you?'

Quinn nodded. 'Maybe it was the age difference—I used to take him places, play games with him. God knows, our father never did. I taught him to ride a bike and to play chess.' Memory darkened his eyes. 'I'd thought about leaving that house for years. I used to tell myself I couldn't because I couldn't leave Alan alone. But the truth was that I knew how badly I'd miss him.'

Paige put down her fork. 'That's not what people think.'

He laughed. 'Yes, I know. The proverbial black sheep, that was supposed to be me.' He raised his champagne-glass and watched the bubbles rise. 'I suppose I was, in a way. In the Fowler house, you did as you were told. No questions asked, ever.'

'Yes,' she said softly, thinking of Mrs Fowler's wedding plans and Mr Fowler's decision to send Alan to South America. 'Yes, I know.'

Quinn nodded. 'Alan got the hang of it early. I—I never managed.' He stared into the distance and then took a sip of champagne. 'Look, that's all water under the bridge. I made a lot of mistakes.'

'What mistakes?'

He looked at her through narrowed eyes. 'Do you really want to hear all this?'

She did, she thought suddenly. She wanted to know more about this forceful, mysterious man who had turned her life upside-down.

'Yes,' she said simply.

Quinn stared at her and then he nodded. 'OK,' he said, getting to his feet. 'Why not?' He laughed, but it was less a laugh than a sound of bitter reflection. 'Husbands and wives shouldn't have secrets from each other, should they?' Paige said nothing, and he walked to the french doors and peered into the darkness. 'It's not the world's worst story,' he said. 'I guess I always gave my parents a hard time. My father enrolled me in his preparatory school the day I was born. When I was seventeen, I was politely asked to leave. You can imagine how he loved that. And then I dropped out of college—his *alma mater*, of course. When I asked him to enrole me in a school that offered computer studies, he told me not to be stupid, that there was no future in computers.'

Paige shook her head. 'But you own a computer firm. You said . . .'

'Yes,' he said softly, 'I certainly do.'

'Then, he changed his mind? He agreed to send you to another school?'

'My father and I never agreed about anything,' Quinn said, resting his hands on the mantel and staring into the coals. 'He told me to go back to school and stop making trouble if I wanted his support. Otherwise . . .'

'Otherwise? she prompted.

He shrugged. 'Otherwise, I was on my own. So I found a job—hauling bags of cement,' he said with a quick smile. 'It paid pretty well, for a guy with no training in anything but which fork to use at dinner. And it drove my old man crazy.' The smile came again. 'God, how he hated having me go in and out of that house dressed as a labourer. And my mother . . . "What will people think?" she said. Hell, by the time Alan got himself smashed, I knew I'd been pushing my luck. I should have been long gone by then.'

'Did they really accuse you of getting Alan drunk?'

'Yes. They said I'd always been a bad influence on him.' His eyes darkened. 'Alan cried—he was only a kid. And I . . . I packed a toothbrush and an extra pair of jeans and took off.'

'But—to where? How did you live?'

'It wasn't as bad as it sounds, Paige. I wasn't a baby—I was almost twenty-one. The way I figured it, independence day was long overdue.' He bent and added a log to the fire. 'I must have sent Alan postcards from a hundred different places over the next two years. I worked anywhere they'd have me, at anything they asked.' He grinned. 'The muscles I'd grown working as a labourer grew new muscles. I found out it was tougher to make a living with your hands than your head.'

Paige's glace moved over his shoulders and arms, lingering on the ridged muscles visible beneath his jacket. Yes, she thought, that explained a lot. Everything he'd told her explained a lot. He wasn't a man who had walked out; he was a man who shouldered responsibility, not as a burden but as a mark of pride.

'But you found a way to study computer science,' she said, watching his face.

He nodded. 'I saved every cent I earned. It took me two years, but finally I had enough for a year's tuition at Cal Tech.' He picked up the champagne-bottle and looked at her. 'More?' he asked. She nodded, watching as he refilled her glass. 'After the first year, the school put me on scholarship.' He looked over the rim of his glass and smiled at her. 'The rest, as they say, is history.'

'You got your degree and you went to England and bought your own company.'

He smiled. 'It wasn't quite that simple. I came to the UK, took a look, and decided this was where I wanted to be. I liked the people, the pace of life—and it looked good for computers. They were relatively new, but the American market was already crowded. There seemed a better chance at a future here. But I needed capital, and since I had no collateral, I swallowed my pride and went to my father.'

His words drifted into the silence. Paige reached to him, then drew back her hand before she let herself touch him.

'Did he agree to lend you the money?'

Quinn laughed. 'You sound as surprised as I felt—until he explained his terms.' His voice flattened. 'He lent me the money—but he charged me two per cent over the bank rate.'

'But . . . but that's usury!'

He shrugged. 'What's a father for?' he asked lightly. 'Besides, I paid back every cent within five years—at *three* per cent over the rate.'

She laughed softly. 'I can imagine how that must have felt. As if you'd . . . you'd climbed Everest or gone to the moon or . . .'

Quinn's eyes met hers. 'That's how it felt, all right.'

'And now—are you and your father any closer?'

He grinned. 'Like a cat and a mouse. No, that's not ture. Things are better between us. I let him make it sound as if my success was his. He laughed about throwing me out years before, and about the terms of our loan—he said he'd just been trying to shock me into succeeding. My mother went along with it—I guess that was easier than facing the truth.'

She waited for him to continue, but he said nothing. 'Have you any regrets?' she asked finally. 'I mean, do you ever miss home?'

Quinn laughed. 'This is my home,' he said, making a broad gesture that she knew included more than the house. 'I've been back to the States on business, but I hadn't been in Connecticut in years. Not until Alan called and told me about . . .'

His face changed, closed in on itself. For a few minutes, they had both forgotten the reason they'd met. Now, looking at him, Paige knew their fragile peace had been shattered.

'You're a woman of many talents,' he said softly. 'I never would have dreamed you could do such a credible job of pretending to listen to a story that isn't terribly interesting.'

'I wasn't pretending,' she said quickly. 'And it was interesting. It explains things about you.'

He put down his champagne-glass. 'What things?'

'Just—things. I mean, you're so different from Alan.'

It had been the wrong thing to say. She could see it in the sudden tilt of his head.

'That's right, Paige,' he murmured, taking the glass from her nerveless fingers. 'I'm nothing like my brother.'

Her heart hammered crazily. 'Quinn, please . . .'

'Is this how you strung him along, Paige? Cosy chit-chat, questions about his childhood . . .'

'That's not what I was doing.'

'I'm not that easily distracted.' His lips drew away from his teeth. 'And I'm not half as patient.'

'Quinn . . .'

'If I put my ring on a woman's finger, I expect to make love to her.'

How could he change so quickly? Paige stared at his

angry face. Moments ago, she'd glimpsed the man she'd
met at the Hunt Club Ball. Now, he was someone else, dark
and frightening.

'Don't,' she whispered.

But it was too late. He had already drawn her into his
arms. 'You're wearing my wedding ring,' he said softly.
'Now, what do you think that means?' Her pulse leaped as
his eyes swept over her. 'Hell,' he said, 'I've waited too long
as it is.'

'No . . .'

He gathered her to him and his mouth descended on hers,
muffled her cry. She felt the bite of his teeth, the thrust of
his tongue, as she stood rigid within his angry embrace.

'Come on,' he growled. 'Don't play games with me.'

Tears glistened in her eyes. Quinn stared at her, and then
he muttered an oath.

'Don't cry,' he said roughly. 'Juliet . . .'

The name brought with it a sweet rush of memories. He
had remembered, too. She saw it in the way he looked at
her. And then the pulsing brightness in the sea-depths of
his eyes dulled, and she knew that although she had
remembered a moment of magic, he had remembered
treachery.

His mouth covered hers as he swept her up into his arms
and moved swiftly out of the library and up the stairs. The
house swirled around her as it had the night before. Last
night, exhausted and frightened, Quinn's arms had offered
solace. Tonight, his embrace was a reminder of what lay
ahead. This long climb into darkness would not end in
quiet sleep. It would end in the tangle of Quinn's bed, in
the fierceness of his anger and possession.

She cringed as his shoulder slammed against the bedroom
door. It flew open, banging against the wall as he strode
across the room and lowered her to the bed. His body
followed hers, covering her with its hard demand. When he

spoke, his voice was a harsh whisper in the darkness.

'No more games, Paige,' he whispered. 'It's pay-off time.'

He reached across her and switched on the table-lamp. Light blazed across them, washing them in cold, white brilliance. Quinn's hands moved on her with feverish haste, cupping her breasts, tracing the curve of her hip, learning the long line of leg and thigh that lay hidden beneath her velvet dress. The touch that had made her flame with desire only days before now made her cringe in fear.

Her thoughts fled to the only other time she'd lain with a man. It was a memory of pain, of humiliation, of dreams that had died in the face of reality. Nothing could have been worse, she'd thought. But, as Quinn's body moved roughly against hers, she knew she'd been very wrong.

This was worse. This was a perversion of the spell she'd been under that first night in Quinn's arms. He'd seized the magic between them and turned it into a weapon to use against her.

She closed her eyes and lay immobile beneath his rough caresses, and finally he lifted his head and stared down at her.

'Kiss me, damn you,' he said. 'Where's all that fire I remember?' His hand moved over her again, bruising her flesh. 'You wanted me when you thought you'd never have to see me again.' His voice grew rough. 'What's the matter, sweet Juliet? Can't you make it with a man who knows you for what you are?'

'Do it, and have it done with,' she whispered.

She turned her face from his and closed her eyes, crying silently, waiting for the nightmare to end. There was silence, and then the squeak of the springs, and suddenly Quinn was standing beside the bed.

'Look at me, Paige.' Slowly, unwillingly, she focused her tear-stained eyes on him. A lock of dark hair hung over his forehead. His jacket was in disarray, his shirt opened half-way down his chest. 'It won't work,' he said in a harsh whisper. 'You think you can reduce me to something less than human, to a man who takes a woman while she lies beneath him in silence.' His eyes blazed in his pale face. 'But I won't accommodate you.' He bent suddenly and caught her by the shoulders, lifting her roughly towards him. 'Sooner or later, you're going to need a man, just the way you did the night we met. And when you do, I'll be here. I'll make love to you until you beg me to stop. And then . . .'

Her eyes fixed on his face. 'And then?' she whispered. She didn't want to hear the rest, but she knew she must.

Quinn's hands cut into her flesh before he flung her back against the pillow. 'And then, damn you, I'll be free of you at last.'

CHAPTER EIGHT

IT WAS amazing how two people living in one small house could avoid each other if they really put their minds to it. The day after he almost raped her, Quinn moved his things to the guest-room, and after that Paige saw him hardly at all.

At first, the sound of his footsteps outside her door made the breath catch in her throat. But his pace never faltered. He was gone by the time she came down in the mornings, and he never returned until late—after ten, usually—which made the evening arrangements simple. Paige dined at seven, and at nine she went to her room. On the rare occasions they met in the hall or at the door, he was coldly proper. At least the violence unleashed between them had accomplished something, even if it was only an armed truce.

A week went by, then two. Sometimes, Paige thought it was as if Quinn had forgotten she existed. But that was impossible. He had to be as aware of her presence as she was of his. It couldn't please him to live this way—trapped, with a stranger, in his own home.

Against her own better judgement, she began to hope for release. Quinn was not a fool; sooner or later, he'd have to admit that this mockery of marriage was pointless, and then he'd set her free. He had to. It was the only thing that made sense. Her hopes grew as the days passed—and then, one morning, they came crashing down around her.

She was hurrying to a lecture at the British Museum. Exploring the city, which had begun as a way to pass the days, had rapidly become a passion. London was a wonderful place, she thought as she buttoned her raincoat. No wonder Quinn had chosen to live here. She could be happy here, too, if only—if only . . .

'Mrs Fowler? I'm glad I caught you before you left.'

Paige turned towards the housekeeper in surprise. Norah was far too well-trained to comment on her employer's sleeping arrangements, but since Quinn had moved into the guest-room she'd treated Paige with polite indifference.

'I'm running late, Norah. Can't it wait?'

Norah shook her head. 'It's about the dinner party on Saturday night.'

Paige looked at the woman blankly. 'Dinner party?'

'Yes, ma'am. Will it be a buffet or a sit-down? If you want a sit-down, we'll need extra help in the dining-room. I can arrange it, if you like, but the caterer likes to have a few days' notice.'

Paige shook her head. 'I don't know anything about Mr Fowler's plans for Saturday,' she said. 'You'll have to ask him.'

'I did. He said such things were for you to decide. There'll be six for dinner. Will you want drinks and canapés first, or . . .'

'You've made an error,' Paige said stiffly. 'This has nothing to do with me.'

The housekeeper shook her head. 'I've made no error, ma'am.' Her eyes met Paige's. 'Believe me, Mrs Fowler, I was as surprised as you.'

A flush crept up Paige's cheeks. 'Very well, Norah,' she said quietly. 'I'll take care of it.'

The strange conversation haunted her all day. What did it mean? She knew Quinn entertained out-of-town clients every now and then; she'd overheard him telephoning the Connaught hotel several times, making dinner arrangements. But he never brought guests home, and even if he had she had no role in such plans. Surely Norah had misunderstood Quinn's instructions? Paige saw no alternative but to confront him and ask him to straighten things out with his housekeeper.

She was waiting for him in the sitting-room that night when he returned home. She rose when she heard his key in the lock, mouth dry, heart pounding.

Don't be such a fool, she told herself, and she took a breath and stepped into the doorway.

'Quinn? I'd like to talk to you for a moment.'

Her nose wrinkled as he followed her into the sitting-room. There was a faint smell of whisky about him and something else mixed with it, something vaguely floral.

'What is it?' he asked without ceremony.

Paige swallowed. 'Norah came to me with questions about a dinner you were planning. I told her she was mistaken.'

'She was not mistaken,' he said, crossing the room to the cellaret in the corner. 'There'll be six, including you and me. I thought we'd have something informal, but the final decision is yours.'

Paige looked at him in surprise as he poured himself a brandy. 'But . . . but that's out of the question, Quinn. You and I don't . . . we have no reason to plan a dinner or . . .'

He tossed off the amber liquid in one swallow. 'We have every reason. We're married, Paige.' His cool gaze moved over her slowly. 'This is our house. I pay the bills. What, precisely, do you?'

Don't rise to the bait, she thought. 'I've been thinking of going to an agency and looking for a job.'

Quinn laughed. 'They don't advertise for women with your skills, sweetheart.'

'Damn you, Quinn.'

He set the brandy snifter down on the bar. 'You have a job,' he said harshly. 'You're my wife.'

Her anger faded beneath the pulse of fear in her blood. 'I thought we'd settled that.'

He crossed the room and took hold of her shoulders. 'Settled it?' he asked softly. The smell of whisky was stronger, and she realised he'd been drinking long before he had the brandy. 'No, sweet Juliet, we have not settled it.' His mouth curved into a cruel smile. 'We will, though. Some day soon. I promise.'

'You've been drinking,' she said coldly.

His eyes narrowed. 'What I do is my business.'

Paige nodded. 'Exactly. And so is your dinner party. I won't . . .

She gasped as his grip on his tightened. 'You bloody well will! I've spent the past weeks like a stranger in my own home, and I don't like it.' His hands fell to his sides. 'It's time you paid your way here. I expect you to dine with me in the evenings.'

'What for? You and I . . .'

'You and I are married,' he growled. 'That means we're going to dine together, talk together, be seen together. I'm weary of making excuses about where my bride keeps herself. It's been my habit to entertain in my home.' He smiled coldly. 'It's going to be hard to do that with you in your room while my guests and I dine.'

'All that has nothing to do with me.'

'It's time you lived up to our contract and started playing the part of my loving wife.' He looked into her eyes. 'Surely someone with your talent can manage that.'

'That's impossible. You can't expect . . .'

'I can and do expect, Paige. Civility is a small enough price to pay for the money I deposit to your bank account, isn't it?'

She felt her face blaze beneath his mocking smile. Finally, she nodded stiffly.

'All right. What is it you want me to do?'

His smile faded and she thought, for a heartstopping moment, he was going to take her into his arms. Her breath quickened; it had been so long since he'd touched her, yet she could still remember the feel of his body, the taste of his mouth. But all he did was brush his hand lightly along her cheek.

'Only what you can, sweet Juliet.' His voice was soft, with a quality of fatigue that she'd never expected, and her eyes lifted slowly to his.

'Quinn,' she whispered.

'What is it, Paige?'

'I . . . I . . .' She looked at him in confusion. What had she wanted to say say to him? 'I . . . I'll do what you want.'

His eyes grew dark. 'Will you?' he said slowly, and then the coldness she'd come to know so well returned to his face. 'You can start by joining me for breakfast tomorrow. We can talk about the dinner party then.'

Paige nodded. 'All right.' Quinn turned away, and the floral scent drifted to her again. Suddenly, she felt as if a fist had clamped around her heart.

Perfume. A woman's perfume . . .

Not that it mattered. He could be with whomever he wished. But Paige lay awake half that night, tormented by images of a nameless woman lying sated with passion in her husband's arms.

She joined him the next morning and again that night at dinner. They sat opposite each other in silence, like strangers sharing a table in a café, until Quinn put down his teacup and looked at her.

'It's going to be difficult to carry on a conversation with guests present if we know nothing about each other,' he said.

'We have nothing to say,' Paige answered stiffly.

Quinn's expression was grim. 'Then we'll find something.'

Their first talks were stilted discussions of weather and current affairs. It became easier when they discovered a common love of political cartoons. And then, one morning, Paige asked about a book of photos she'd found in the library.

'Are they yours?'

Quinn nodded. 'I've been a camera buff for years. I'm not very good . . .'

'You are,' she said quickly, and then her cheeks flushed. 'I mean, I don't know much about photography, but there's a quality to your pictures that's very moving.'

A pleased smile curved across his lips. 'Well,' he said softly, 'thank you.' And he offered to show her his basement darkroom. Paige, whose knowledge of film began and ended with the fact that it came neatly packaged in little yellow boxes, entered the small, red-lit room warily. She emerged a convert, convinced that what went on in all those chemical baths was a miracle.

The next day—a Saturday—Quinn was again silent at breakfast. Paige had almsot decided their truce of the past week had ended, when he suddenly put down his cup and stared at her.

'I'm going to Hyde Park to take pictures,' he said, rushing the words together. 'There's a kite festival, and . . .' His eyes sought hers. 'Would you care to come along? You don't have to, of course . . .'

'I'd like to. Very much,' Paige said quickly, and she smiled at him in a way she never had before. 'Thank you for asking me.'

Later, she would remember the day as some kind of turning-point. Quinn shot off three rolls of film, and then he bought a kite from a vendor and within minutes a shiny blue and red dragon was soaring over their heads. They laughed like children, feeding the dragon yards of string, watching as it sailed above the treetops. When the wind suddenly plucked the string from Paige's fingers, she was desolate.

'I've lost it! Oh, Quinn, I'm sorry.'

'I'm not,' he said softly, smiling at her. 'It's been a lovely day.'

She felt her face glow and she told herself it was from the kiss of the chilled air. But, when it was time to leave, it seemed natural for their fingers to lace together as they walked to his car.

It was impossible to notice all the ways in which they opened to each other after that. Paige only knew that, somewhere along the way, the day improved the moment Quinn arrived home. They rarely went out to dinner, preferring to have it in the quiet of the library. On Norah's evenings off, Paige insisted on cooking.

'I like to fuss in the kitchen,' she said, and when Quinn solemnly complimented her on some simple meal, her heart filled with joy.

After dinner, they sat by the fire. They read. Quinn taught Paige chess, cheering her when she won her first game, although she had a strong suspicion he'd let her win. They went to concerts at the Barbican, to the theatre, and one drizzle evening they walked slowly through quiet Mayfair, huddled together comfortably under an umbrella.

They talked about everything—except what had brought them together in the first place. Paige wanted to talk about that. She wanted to expose the past for what it was—a dark set of circumstances forced on them by others, but she was hesitant. One evening, she finally broached the subject.

'I spoke with my father today,' she said. 'He says he's grateful . . .'

Quinn's eyes flashed a warning. 'I don't want his gratitude or anybody else's,' he said, and he turned away from her. 'How was your day?' he asked after a moment, and she was quick to fall in with his obvious effort to change the emotionally charged subject.

It was worse when she mentioned Alan. When a letter from him arrived, Quinn took it into the library and closed the door. Paige searched his face anxiously when he came out.

'How is Alan?' she asked when she couldn't bear the silence another moment.

'Fine.'

'Is he . . .'

'I don't want to discuss Alan,' he said sharply. 'Do you understand?'

She told herself she did. Their relationship had improved, but it was still tenuous. There was no point in opening old wounds. In the dark of night, a silent voice warned that ignoring things wasn't the same as coming to terms with them. But her niggling doubts seemed foolish by daylight.

What counted was that she and Quinn were getting along with each other. Of course, they were only doing all this so that she could carry off her public duties as his wife. And yet, except for that first dinner party, they saw no one but each other. It was as if they were living in their own world, brought to life by the sound of Quinn's key in the door at night.

Paige found herself glancing at her watch each afternoon, wondering if he'd be early or late. Early meant around six; he was never home sooner than that. By then, she always had the fire started in the library and her clothes changed. One chill autumn afternoon, she'd laid the fire and was just hurrying upstairs when she heard the door open and close.

She paused half-way up the stairs. 'You're home,' she said foolishly, staring at Quinn in surprise as he stood in the doorway looking up at her. He was looking at her strangely, and she ran her hand through her hair a bit self-consciously. 'I only just got in,' she said. 'I was at the Victoria and

Albert and I got caught in the rain . . .' God, she was babbling! But he was making her nervous, watching her like that. 'I didn't realise it was so late.'

Quinn's smile was slight. 'I came home early. I thought it would be nice if we went for a drive before dinner.'

Why was he staring at her? There was something different about him tonight, but what? Paige swallowed past the sudden dryness in her throat.

'I'd like that,' she said carefully. 'Just give me a minute to change . . .' The look on his face stopped her. 'Fine,' she said. 'Let's go.'

In the enclosed space of the Jaguar, the easy informality that had grown between them over the weeks vanished. Their conversation was stilted, and when they stopped for dinner at an Elizabethan pub beside the Thames, it all but disappeared.

'This is a handsome old place, isn't it?' Quinn asked after they'd ordered and the silence had stretched on and on.

Paige nodded. 'Yes, it's lovely.'

'Would you like some more wine?'

'No, thanks,' she said politely.

More silence. When their meal arrived, it was a welcome distraction, but Paige could hardly manage a mouthful and, when Quinn suggested they leave, she almost knocked her chair over in her rush to get to her feet.

'It's late,' he said curtly, and she nodded in agreement, for once eager to reach the solitude of her own bedroom. She breathed a sigh of relief when they finally reached the house again. Something had gone wrong, but she hadn't the slightest idea what it was.

The door closed behind them. 'Goodnight,' she said at the foot of the stairs. 'Thank you for . . .'

'Would you like some brandy?'

Paige shook her head. 'No, thanks. I . . . I think I'll call it a night.'

Quinn nodded. 'I'll see you up.'

She almost told him that was silly, that she lived in his house and slept in a room down the hall from his, but something in his voice warned her not to argue, and she nodded and started up the stairs. He followed behind her; a pulse began to beat in her throat as she thought of him watching the movement of her hips and legs. When they reached the second floor, she hurried to the closed door of her room.

'Goodnight,' she said, turning towards him.

'Paige,' he said, his voice a husky whisper. 'Paige . . .'

Everything seemed to happen with an unreal slowness. She looked up at him and saw the dark fire in his eyes. And when he put his hand on her arm, she suddenly understood everything. The electric awareness that had brought them together seemed to pulse in the charged air.

Quinn wanted her. And she wanted him. The weeks of being together had been leading them to this all along; he had just realised it before she had. That was why he'd come home early, that was the reason for the tension all evening.

She turned away in confusion. His arms closed around her and he drew her back against him, whispering her name again. The sound of it lay thick as honey on his tongue.

Paige felt the press of his body, hard and solid, against hers. Her eyes closed and she let herself lean back against him, resting her weight on his chest and encircling arms. She could feel the heat of him spreading over her, smell the scent that was his alone. His lips brushed her hair and a tremor raced through her. The next step was hers. All she had to do was turn to him, lift her mouth to his . . .

You're going to need a man—and I'll be here.

The ugly words leaped into her mind. But Quinn had said that before they knew each other. Surely it was all different now?

I'll make love to you until you beg me to stop. And then

I'll be free of you at last.

She felt as if a cold hand had clamped over her heart. 'It's late, Quinn,' she said. 'And I'm tired.'

'Juliet . . .'

She closed her eyes, grateful that he couldn't see her face. 'Please,' she whispered.

His fingers bit into her shoulders and then his hands slid from her.

'Yes, of course,' he said, and suddenly she was alone in the hallway.

He was gone by the time she came down to breakfast the next morning. It was the first time in weeks that they hadn't begun the day together, and she was surprised at how empty the house seemed without him. When the phone rang at mid-morning, she snatched it up, smiling when she heard Quinn's voice.

'I missed you this morning,' she said before she had time to think.

There was a silence. 'I told Norah to let you sleep in,' he said after a while. 'You said you were tired last night.'

Paige swallowed. 'Quinn, about last night...'

'Forget it,' he said brusquely. 'It's tonight I want to talk about. A client's in town—his wife wants to attend a concert at Albert Hall.'

'Do you want me to arrange for tickets?'

He sighed. 'They insist on company, Paige. I tried to talk them out of it, but—look, would you mind very much if we went along with them? This guy's a pain, but he's placing an enormous software order, and . . .'

'I don't mind at all,' she said quickly, grateful for the safe company of strangers. 'Shall I meet you?'

His voice softened. 'Thanks, Paige. See you tonight.'

She dressed for the evening with more care than usual. By the time she left the house, she was running late. When she stepped from a taxi outside the Albert Hall, she looked around eagerly for Quinn. Crowds milled about the steps that led to the building, but it took only a moment to see that he wasn't there yet. There would be no mistaking his presence—they were attuned to each other again, just as they had been the night they'd meet at the All Hallows Ball. Her heart tripped over. Quinn, she thought, Quinn . . .

She started as an arm slid around her waist. Quinn smiled down at her.

'Hello,' she said. 'I didn't see you coming. I must have been daydreaming.'

He grinned. 'That's an understatement. You looked as if you were a million miles away. What were you thinking about?'

About last night, when I was foolish enough to step out of your arms and send you away.

The realisation came with stunning swiftness. Somehow, she managed a little laugh.

'I was wondering if you were ever going to get here,' she said. 'What's your client going to say if we're late?'

Quinn sighed as he led her towards the door. 'We're not late enough,' he murmured, glancing at the tickets in his hand. 'They've yet to begin.'

'What an awful thing to say,' she whispered for the benefit of the ticket taker, but it was impossible to keep a straight face, and she began to laugh. There was something about laughing with him, she thought, looking at his smiling face. Her heart soared. Everything was wonderful, when she was at his side. 'Actually, I agree. It's Mahler tonight, isn't it? God, I hate Mahler!'

Quinn nodded. 'Only Jack Ward likes Gustav,' he said. Paige looked at him and he made a face. 'The client we're meeting inside.'

'Ah, yes, the man who's going to commission a million billion computer programs.' She shuddered as the discordant strains of the Fifth Symphony reached out to them.

'I guess it's going to be a long evening.'

'Longer than you think,' Quinn said with a sigh. 'If you think the music's a bore, wait until you meet good old Jack.' He smiled as he led her ito the Hall. 'But I guess I can put up with him for one night. Let's hope he plans on placing the biggest order the company's ever had.'

What 'good old Jack' planned on, Paige thought grimly later that evening, was making a quick move on her. When she and Quinn took their seats, protocol placed Quinn beside Mrs Ward and Paige beside the woman's husband. There had been some swift introductions—Ward himself was a tall man with a handsome face and a shock of thick, fair hair. His wife had a sweet expression and sad eyes. It was all there was time to notice before the music began again.

At first, Paige thought it was her imagination when Jack Ward's hand brushed her thigh. She glanced at him out of the corner of her eye. Of course it had been her imagination. His face, set in rapt concentration, was turned to the orchestra. Five minutes later, his programme fell to the floor. 'Sorry,' he muttered as he reached for it. This time, his hand brushed Paige's breast. 'Sorry,' he said again.

By the time the concert ended, there were half a dozen more 'sorries', and Paige hadn't believed one of them. No one could have that many 'accidents'. Ward's foot touched hers, his leg brushed hers, and when they piled into a taxi on their way to a supper club, his thigh rubbed her thigh.

And there was nothing she could do about it. His actions were too swift and subtle. She'd met men like Ward before, and she knew how the game worked. If she said something, told him to keep his hands to himself, he'd deny having done anything. The only loser would be Quinn. Ward would certainly never do business with his company after she'd made a scene.

Mrs Ward wouldn't gain anything, either. Paige's heart went out to the woman. No wonder she had such sad eyes—she knew exactly what her husband was doing; she'd probably lived through this kind of embarrassment before. She kept casting apologetic looks at Paige, as if to tell her she was sorry. Calling Jack in on his nasty little game would only heap further humiliation on the poor woman's head.

She wondered what Quinn would do if he knew what was happening. Flatten Ward's nose, perhaps. The thought gave her a certain amount of satisfaction. When they were alone later, she'd tell Quinn that Ward wasn't only a bore, he was a boor. Perhaps she'd offer to make some tea when they got back to the house. Better yet, Quinn might suggest a brandy as he had last night. 'Yes,' she'd say, and let the magic of All Hallows Eve reclaim them.

She looked up. Quinn was watching her; she could feel the heat of his gaze. Beneath the table, Ward was moving his foot against hers in a steady rhythm, but she was unaware of it. She was conscious only of Quinn. His eyes were hooded, unreadable. Her cheeks flamed. What was he thinking? What was behind that dark intensity?

'. . . tell your fortune.'

She blinked. 'What? Did you say something, Mr Ward?'

The man smiled wetly. 'It's Jack, sweetie. I said, if you give me your hand, I'll tell your fortune. An old gypsy taught me.'

'No, thank you very much, Mr Ward, I . . .'

Ward grasped her hand and drew it towards him. 'Come on, don't be such a stick. Let's take a look at your love line.'

Paige looked up again. Ward was still talking, but she had tuned him out. Quinn was listening to Mrs Ward, his head bent attentively towards hers. Why had she ever thought his mouth hard? she wondered. It wasn't hard at all, it was sensual. And his eyes—there was nothing cold about them.

They were the colour of the sea, yes, but it was the southern sea, where the water sometimes felt as warm as blood.

Quinn's head turned slowly towards her. His eyes settled on her face, on her mouth. She felt the heat of his gaze, and she touched her tongue slowly to her lips in an unconscious acknowledgment of desire. A terrible look stole over Quinn's face. Was he angry? No, he couldn't be.

She blinked again. 'For heaven's sake, Mr Ward,' she said irritably, pulling her hand free. 'Don't do that.'

'Do what?' Ward asked innocently.

Paige shuddered and wiped her hand against a napkin. She'd been concentrating so hard on Quinn that it had taken her a while to realise that Ward was running his index finger along her palm. Some day, she wanted the pleasure of telling him that it wasn't a sexy gesture when he did it; she felt as if a snail had crawled across her flesh and left a slimy trail behind. But not tonight. Tonight, she was too busy with the flood of discoveries she was making about Quinn. About her husband.

'Come on, sweetie. Let's show these two what dancing's all about.'

Ward pulled her chair from the table and, before Paige could protest, she was locked in his arms and they were moving across the dance-floor.

'I don't really feel like dancing,' she said, trying to hold her body away from his. 'Please, Mr Ward . . .'

'Jack,' he said again. 'Why are you so stiff, lovey? Didn't anybody ever teach you to dance?'

'I'm not stiff,' she said grimly. 'I just don't like to be held so closely.'

But she forgot about Ward when she saw Quinn over his shoulder. He had led Mrs Ward out to the middle of the dance-floor. She watched as his arms went around the woman and they began to move to the music. Quinn held her at a polite distance, but Paige felt a tight knot of jealousy balloon beneath her breast. He hadn't danced with her at all. This was her third dance with 'good old Jack', and Quinn's second with Mrs Ward, but . . .

Jack's embrace tightened, and Paige pushed against him. 'Don't do that,' she said irritably.

'Come on, dearie. You can be nicer than that.'

'I said, don't do that,' she repeated. Ward smelled of sweat and cigars, and he was holding her much too closely. What a fool she'd been, she thought suddenly. Quinn would never have wanted her to let Ward paw her, not for any number of orders. He was too decent, too good, too caring . . .

Ward pulled her against him. 'Stop it,' she snapped, and, as she put her hands on his chest and tried pushing him from her, his feet tangled with hers. Paige stumbled, clinging to Ward's neck to keep from falling.

'That's the girl,' he said, wrapping his arms around her waist.

The press of his body against hers was sickening. 'Let go of me.'

'Don't go all coy and girlish on me now,' he whispered, and she felt the wet brush of his mouth on her cheek. His body ground against hers again. 'Why don't you meet me at my hotel tomorrow, hmm? I'll send the wife out shopping for a couple of hours. I'll . . .' His voice rose in alarm. 'Hey! What's going on?'

Paige's eyes widened as Jack Ward fell away from her. Quinn had appeared from out of nowhere, and he stood between them, unmoving, unsmiling, as if he'd been carved of stone.

'We're leaving,' he said to Paige. His voice was quiet, his eyes on her steady and dark. 'Get your things.'

'What the hell is this, Fowler? Your wife . . .'

Ward's face paled as Quinn's hand tightened on his arm.

'Exactly,' he said in a malice-filled voice. '*My* wife, Ward. Not yours. Not anyone's. She belongs to me.'

She belongs to me. A tremor raced along Paige's skin. During the past couple of weeks, she'd forgotten that deadly possessiveness. It had frightened her that first day in London; now, it thrilled her. She *did* belong to him, and it was what she wanted. It was what she'd always wanted.

Quinn's eyes slid to hers. 'How long has he been pawing you?'

Paige swallowed. 'Quinn, it's all right. I . . .'

'Did you hear what she said, Fowler? I . . .'

Quinn's eyes flashed. 'I asked my wife the question, Ward. Not you.' He looked at Paige. 'Answer me,' he said. 'Has it been going on all night?'

'Yes. But . . .'

'Why didn't you tell me?'

She looked at Ward's pale face. 'I thought about it. But he's your client. He . . .'

'Mr Ward,' Quinn said with sarcastic deliberation, 'is a son of a bitch, and he's lucky I don't slam his head through the wall. Now, get your things and meet me at the door.'

Paige nodded and moved quickly past Jack Ward. She could almost smell the man's fear, and she couldn't blame him for it. Quinn was a formidable enemy. To face his anger was terrifying. But he wasn't angry at her; he'd only sounded that way. He had no reason to be angry at her, unless . . .

Has it been going on all night?

Why didn't you tell me?

Mrs Ward looked up as Paige reached their table and took her things from the chair.

'I'm sorry,' Paige began, and the woman shook her head.

'Don't worry about it,' she said with weary resignation.

'Jack's always been like that. He never thinks anybody knows what he's up to.' She looked across the dance-floor to where Quinn and her husband still stood. 'Your man's going to cramp his style for a while, anyway. Jack looks as if he might die of fear.'

Paige nodded. There was nothing she could think of that seemed right to say, and by now she could see Quinn striding towards the door. She hurried towards him, watching as he stuffed a handful of banknotes into their waiter's hand.

His arm slid around her when she reached him. He held her so tightly that she almost cried out. But being held against him was a comfort. She looked up at him as they stepped out into the dark night.

'Poor Mrs Ward,' she said. 'I feel so sorry for her.'

There was no answer. Quinn opened the door of the Jaguar and she slipped into the seat, watching as he came around the car and got in beside her.

'She said he's done that sort of thing before. She said she hopes you cramped his style. She . . .'

Metal ground against metal as he jammed the car into gear and pulled away from the kerb.

'I'm delighted that Mrs Ward approved of my behaviour.'

Paige looked at him. His voice was filled with cold anger. She reached across the console and put her hand on his as it lay on the steering wheel. It was the first time she'd ever touched him of her own volition.

'Quinn,' she said hesitantly, 'are you—are you angry with me?'

His lips drew back from his teeth. 'Why should I be?'

His answer was the one she wanted. But there was something in the way he'd given it that made her uncomfortable. She looked at him and then at the dark street. What she needed was a hot shower. She could still feel the slither of Ward's hands on her, and the memory made her shudder. Yes, a shower first. And then . . . and then . . .

Her heart turned over, and she glanced at Quinn shyly. What would happen between them tonight? She trembled as she thought of those breathless moments in his arms the night before. Yes, she thought, yes, it would be like that again. Only, this time she wouldn't send him away. This time . . .

The Jaguar slid to the kerb in the silent mews. Quinn shut off the engine, and the sounds of the night closed around them. Paige's mouth was dry with anticipation.

'Remind me to send good old Jack a box of cigars tomorrow.'

His remark was so unexpected that she laughed. 'Jack?' she said, turning towards him. 'His wife's the one who deserves a gift, not him. A dozen roses, at least, for being so long-suffering.'

Quinn stepped from the car and came around to her side. 'I wonder what kind he smokes?' He held his hand out and Paige took it as she stepped on to the pavement. 'Do you happen to know?'

She looked up at him as his arm encircled her waist. 'How would I know what Mr Ward smokes, Quinn? I don't know why you'd send him anything, after what he did.'

The front door slammed shut behind them, and Quinn pressed her back against it. His hands cupped her face and tilted it to his.

'Come on, sweetheart, we both know what he did,' he said in that soft, dangerous voice she knew so well. 'Good old Jack got you warmed up.' His teeth flashed whitely. 'He deserves a little something for that, don't you think?'

She froze. 'Got me warmed . . . ? Quinn, what are you talking about?'

His arms closed around her. 'You must think I'm blind,' he growled. 'But why wouldn't you? Hell, I acted as if I were, these past weeks.'

Her eyes rounded with disbelief. 'These past weeks were wonderful. They . . .'

'I'll bet they were. How does playing at being Mrs Quinn Fowler feel?' She gasped as his fingers dug into her flesh. 'What's it like, playing a game by your own rules, darling?'

'No,' she whispered, 'it . . . it wasn't like that, Quinn. You know . . .'

'I know what I saw tonight,' he snarled. 'You have no shame, have you? Coming on to Ward in front of his wife, in front of me . . .'

Paige shook her head. 'No. It's not true. He . . .'

'Come on, Paige, don't waste my time with lies. I *saw* you. I saw your eyes begin to darken while you played footsie under the table. I saw the tremor that you couldn't keep from your lips when he caressed your hand.' Distaste twisted his mouth. 'Jesus, the way you ground against him on the dance-floor . . .'

She stared into his face, waiting for him to laugh and tell her it was all a dreadful joke. But his eyes blazed with fury. There had to be a way to make him understand.

'Quinn, I beg you—listen to me. Ward forced himself on me. He . . .'

'The way I did, right, baby?' The sound of his laugher turned her blood to ice. 'Hell, let's not let all his efforts go to waste, Paige.'

She cried out as he swung her up into her arms. 'What are you doing? Quinn . . .'

His arms tightened around her. 'We've said too many goodnights at my bedroom door, sweet Juliet,' he said softly. His mouth swooped to hers in a kiss that stole the breath from her. 'Not tonight, Paige.' His voice roughened as he stared up the dark stairs. 'Tonight, you're not going to send me away.'

CHAPTER NINE

'QUINN, no . . .'

Her cry was silenced by his kiss. His mouth bruised hers as his arms locked her to him. Helpless against his rage, Paige could do nothing except beat her fists against his shoulders as he carried her through the darkness.

How could things change so quickly? Moments ago, she'd been filled with anticipation of what lay ahead. Now, fear sent her pulse racing. This couldn't happen. Not now. Not when they were so close to finally capturing again what had begun between them that long-ago night.

A path of moonlight arrowed from the bedroom door to Quinn's bed, the bed in which she'd slept alone for so many nights. He dropped her into its centre and looked down at her.

'Quinn,' she said quickly, 'listen to me. I . . .'

He opened his jacket and turned away. 'Get your clothes off.'

His voice was rough, the words flat with menace. She watched as he walked to the door, slammed it shut and locked it. The message was clear, and it sent a wave of fear rippling through her.

Nothing would stop him tonight.

Slowly, he began walking towards her. She could see pinpricks of icy light dancing in the stones that were his eyes. He loosened his tie, then undid the top button of his shirt.

'Get undressed, dammit.'

Paige scrambled back against the headboard. 'Quinn, for

God's sake—listen to me. You can't think I was flirting with that man. You can't still think I'm . . .'

'Flirting?' He laughed. 'Is that what you call it?' He shrugged his jacket from his shoulders and tossed it aside. 'Come on,' he said, 'we're wasting time.'

'I'll call for Norah.'

He laughed again. 'Norah's gone to visit her sister.'

She swallowed past the lump in her throat. 'If you're trying to frighten me, Quinn . . .'

His eyes fixed on her face. 'You're wasting your breath, Paige. Get your clothes off and make it fast.'

'What about us?' she whispered. 'You can't pretend . . .'

'Us? *Us?*' The cold smile vanished. 'The only "us" there could possibly be is in that bed—and you've done one hell of a job keeping me out of it.'

Tears filled her eyes. 'Quinn, I beg you . . .'

His voice cut across hers. 'You *will* beg me, before this night ends.'

With a certainty that chilled her, Paige knew that he was telling the truth. In one lithe motion, she rolled across the bed and to the other side. She was quick but he was quicker, and he was on her before she'd taken a step, his hands clamped tightly to her shoulders.

'We can do this the easy way or the hard way,' he said, the words purring with malice. 'Do you like it a little rough? is that it? Hell, I can oblige, if that's what you want.'

Cruelty came so easily to him. How had she forgotten that? Anger began to displace the fear, not just at Quinn but at herself.

'You can't do this, damn you! There are laws . . .'

'Against what? I'm your husband, Paige. What court would deny me the right to sleep with my wife?' His hands clasped her shoulders and he pulled her against him. 'I told you I'd be here when you wanted a man,' he whispered. 'Well, here I am, baby. Ready and able.'

'Quinn, please . . .'

'What's the matter, Paige? I turned you on when we met.' His eyes blazed into hers and he laughed. 'Don't tell me you've forgotten the charm of that evening. It was so old-fashioned, so romantic.'

Colour flooded her cheeks. 'It was wrong. I know that. But I felt . . . I'd never . . .'

His hands fell from her. 'Save your breath,' he growled. 'I remember the whole act.' Slowly, his eyes never leaving hers, he began to unbutton his shirt. 'Watching you with Jack Ward was an encore performance.' The shirt fell open, revealing the dark hair on his muscled chest. 'No wonder he fell all over you.'

'I didn't do . . .'

He grinned wolfishly as he threw the shirt and aside. 'Hell, it's a good act. A beautiful woman convinces a guy that she's on fire, and wouldn't he just like to play fireman.' The terrible smile faded from his face. 'I'll bet it's never failed you yet.'

'I told you, I'd never . . .' Her hands flew to her breast as he reached to her. 'What are you doing?'

'Undressing you,' he said flatly, pushing her hands aside. 'It's what I should have done weeks ago.'

Her mouth turned dry. 'We're not the same people as we were then, Quinn. We . . .'

'We're precisely the same,' he said, while the buttons on her dress opened beneath his fingers. 'We're husband and wife—and we still haven't shared the same bed.'

The dress parted and he pushed it back on her shoulders. His hands curved around her arms and he stared at her.

'How the hell can you look so innocent?' he whispered. 'If only . . .'

A sob caught in her throat as he pulled her to him and kissed her. His lips moved on hers, demanding response. But she felt nothing. Once, Quinn had held her in his arms and the heat of a thousand suns had blazed in her blood. Now, the chill that had held her captive for so long was reclaiming her heart.

Tears stung her eyes. What dark Fate had sent Quinn to her? He was the man who'd freed her from her prison of ice—and now he would be the one who returned her to it for ever.

He lifted his head and looked down at her. His breathing was ragged, his eyes cold stars.

'Playing the Snow Queen won't stop me tonight, Paige.' His fingers played idly with the lace border of her chemise. 'You might as well make it easy on yourself. Pretend I'm Ward. Close your eyes and enjoy it.'

Her heart thudded against her ribs. 'If there's a shred of decency in you . . .'

'Decency?' He cupped her shoulders in his hands and lifted her to her toes. 'Who are you to talk about decency? You don't know the meaning of the word. Christ, if poor Alan had only seen through you. If he'd realised what a scheming bitch you are . . .'

'I wish to God I'd never met your brother,' she sobbed. 'I wish I'd never met you. I . . .'

He growled as he pulled her against him. 'But you did.' His voice held the finality of doom. 'We made an agreement,' he whispered, lowering his head to hers. 'And I'll be damned if I'll let you forget it.'

She stood within his arms like a marble statue. Immobile, cold, beyond feeling, she waited for him to finish what had become inevitable. His lips moved roughly over hers, then to her cheek, her throat, to the shadowed softness of neck and shoulder. She closed her eyes when he caught her chemise and pulled it away from her breasts.

It seemed impossible to remember that she'd ever longed for his caress. But she knew she had; once, the touch of his hands on her skin, the brush of his mouth on hers, had filled her with a rapture so sweet it had made her dizzy with longing. She felt nothing now. It was as if she were elsewhere, watching as Quinn made love to a woman made of stone.

'What is this?'

His voice drew her back. Slowly, she opened her eyes and looked at him. He was looking at her through slitted eyes. His hand was between them, outstretched, the ruby ring he'd given her burning in his palm.

'It's . . . it's the ring you gave me.'

A smile as deadly as summer lightning flashed across his face. 'Yes,' he said. 'I remember.'

He closed his hand over the ring and the length of gold chain from which it hung. The fragile rope drew her closer to him.

'You said it was mine,' she said with a touch of defiance. 'I offered it to you, but you said . . .'

The ring fell from his hand and swung back against her breasts. 'I know what I said. Have you always worn it?'

Her chin lifted. 'I forgot to take it off, that's all.'

'Forgot? All these weeks, and you forgot?' His arms slid around her waist. His breath was warm against her cheek. 'Do you remember the night I gave it to you?'

'No,' she said quickly.

'I do,' he said softly. 'I remember it as if it were yesterday. I told you the flame that burned in the ruby's heart would remind you of me.'

'I . . . I don't remember. I . . .'

His arms tightened around her. 'I said it would make you think of how it would be for us when we made love.'

A tremor raced along her spine. 'That was . . . that was in another lifetime,' she whispered. 'It was . . .'

'Yes,' he said softly, 'it was. It was a time of magic.' He gathered her to him. 'Tell me you remember that night, Paige.'

Her gaze swept over his face, searching it for some new cruelty. His eyes blazed with light, his lips were parted.

'Quinn,' she whispered. 'Quinn . . .'

'Juliet.'

Her eyes closed as his mouth settled on hers. His kiss was gentle, his lips warm and firm. She trembled as his hands cupped her face, tilting it to him. With quick, teasing kisses, he coaxed her mouth open, and his teeth closed lightly on her bottom lip and drew it into the sweet warmth of his mouth.

Paige moaned softly. 'No,' she said, pressing her hands against his chest. 'Please . . .'

'Yes,' he whispered. 'Put your arms around me. Kiss me the way you did that night.' He kissed her again and again, each kiss deeper and more exciting. 'Tell me you want me,' he said against her mouth, and his arms tightened around her. 'Tell me you want to be my wife.'

'I want . . . I want . . .' *I want to be your wife for ever.*

The realisation was raced through her, heating her blood like a current of electricity. Slowly, she lifted her arms to him and whispered his name. Quinn drew in his breath and caught her to him.

'Yes,' he said fiercely, 'yes.'

He lifted her in his arms, then lowered her gently to the bed. Moonlight fell across them, cool and white, as she looked up at him.

'Quinn,' she whispered, 'Quinn . . .'

'Beautiful Paige,' he said thickly, 'my Juliet.'

He whispered to her as he stripped away her clothing, he touched her as he told her things she'd waited a lifetime to hear. She felt her breasts bloom against his hand, felt her nipples bud darkly at the silken brush of his fingers. His lips moved over her throat, her shoulders, and when finally he drew her nipple into his mouth she cried out and clasped him to her.

She whispered his name, and he caught her hand in his and pressed his lips to her palm. 'I've waited so long,' he whispered, folding her fingers over his kiss as if to seal it in her hand for ever. 'All these days and nights, watching you, wanting you . . .'

'Don't leave me,' she said as he rolled away from her.

He touched his hand to her cheek. 'No,' he said softly, 'not tonight.' She watched as he stood beside the bed and stripped off his trousers. His body was lean and powerful, his shoulders broad. She reached out to him as he lay beside her again and took her in his arms, curving her body to the hard length of his.

His mouth covered hers as his hands moved over her, learning all the curves and shadows of her body. She was alive beneath his touch, eager for his kisses, burning with a flame like that which glowed in the heart of the ruby.

The wonder of it made her breathless. She wanted to tell him that what was happening to her was, indeed, magic, that his love had brought her from a cold, dark place into the light—but there was no time for words. And it didn't matter: you didn't need words when you could say so much with a kiss, with a caress, with a sigh.

When he found the centre of her womanhood, Paige pressed her face into his chest and moaned softly. His fingers cupped her, tangling in her moist warmth.

'So lovely,' he murmured. 'So sweet.'

She stiffened when he bent to her. 'No,' she whispered.

But his mouth had already found her, and at his kiss her heart filled with a joy so intense that tears filled her eyes. No one had ever kissed her this way, and no one would, ever again. There would be only Quinn in her arms for the rest of her life. Only Quinn. Only . . .

She cried out as the room spun away from her. He drew her into his arms and held her to him, stroking her flushed cheeks, smoothing the damp hair back from her face,

murmuring soft words to her. After a moment, she touched
him shyly, her palms flat against his chest.

'I . . . I want to . . . to touch you,' she whispered.

'Yes,' he said huskily, and she heard the catch of his
breath as she moved her hand over him. He was all hard
muscle and warm skin. The feel of his body was strange and
exciting. He groaned as she explored the long muscles in his
arms, the length of his spine, and her touch grew bolder.

'Yes,' he murmured again as her fingers traced the curve
of his buttocks. He whispered her name as she touched his
chest again and ran her hand down its length, to the ridged
muscles in his abdomen. She touched his navel, and her
pulse tripped erratically.

'Quinn . . .'

It was a sigh, a question, a desire, and he understood. His
hand closed around her wrist and slowly, gently, he brought
her to him.

His head fell back when her hand closed around him. His
flesh was hard, yet velvet-soft. His warmth was the warmth
of the sun. And he was hers. It was she who had made this
happen.

A swift, fierce joy suffused her. Her arms wound around
his neck as he rolled over her and kissed her deeply.

'Do you want me, Juliet?' he whispered. 'Tell me.'

'Yes,' she said without hesitation. 'Oh, yes. I want you.
Yes . . .'

She wanted to tell him she'd wanted him always, not just
since the night they'd met but since the beginning of time.
But his mouth took hers as he slid his hands beneath her
and lifted her to him, and then it was too late to tell him
anything. She could only call out his name as his passion
filled her with life-giving warmth.

She felt the flutter of wings deep within her as Quinn
began to move, slowly at first, then more quickly, and as his
pace and thrust intensified so did the beat of the wings,

until, in a sudden dazzle of pleasure, Paige broke free of her own body.

The stars, she thought, the stars that blazed in the night sky above the Connecticut shore and the quiet London mews—she could almost grasp them in her hand.

'My Juliet,' Quinn whispered. 'My wife.'

Her heart tumbled with joy, and then the starfire flamed over her and through her. And, as she drifted slowly to earth again, safe in Quinn's arms, she understood the meaning of the oldest magic of all.

Love.

Paige awoke slowly to the patter of rain on the window. Hazy, dream-shot images tumbled through her mind. It was a good morning for dreams, she thought lazily—dreams of starry skies, of strong arms, of Quinn . . .

Quinn. Her heart tumbled wildly. They weren't dreams at all. The long, wonderful night had been real.

She was alone in his bed; she knew that even before she opened her eyes. If he'd been there, she'd have still been locked in his arms as she had been all night, not just when they had made love but when they had slept—although there had been little time for sleep. It was as if Quinn had been determined to make up for all the nights they'd wasted during the weeks of their marriage.

Her cheeks coloured as she thought of the hours gone by, and she smiled as she sat up and ran her hands through her tangled hair. What had become of the woman who froze at a kiss? Paige pushed back the covers and padded barefoot across the bedroom. Out of the corner of her eye, she caught a glimpse of herself in the mirror, and she stopped.

Was that woman with the tousled hair really she? Her mouth looked swollen—she took a step closer and touched her fingers to her lips. Quinn's kisses had done that, she thought in amazement. And the gentle nip of his teeth had left that faint mark on her throat.

She laughed softly as she studied her reflection. The signs of his possession were on her flesh. Her skin seemed to glow with a new radiance, and there was a rosy hue in her cheeks that had never been there before.

The ruby ring no longer lay between her breasts. The delicate chain had broken while they had made love, and the ring lay now on the night-table. Everything was different, she thought, but it was what she felt in her heart that mattered the most. Paige wrapped her arms around herself and twirled in a circle, her bare feet dancing swiftly across the carpeted floor.

I love him. She took a deep breath. 'I love him,' she whispered to the silent room. 'I love him for all time with all my heart.'

She swept up an armful of clothing and dressed quickly. Quinn was waiting for her downstairs. Quinn. Her husband. The realisation made her dizzy with anticipation. Not so long ago, she remembered, she'd stood in this same room, thinking the same thought—but how different that morning had been. She'd hated Quinn then.

No, that wasn't true. She'd never hated him. She'd always loved him, always. Anger and confusion had stood between them, but that was behind them now. She was Quinn's wife. *His wife.* It was what he'd called her all through the night. And today—today, she thought, putting her hand to the doorknob, was the first day of their honeymoon.

The smell of coffee greeted her as she ran down the stairs. The door to the library stood open, but it was empty, as was the small, formal dining-room. Of course—Norah wasn't due back until evening. A quick rush of pink splashed across her cheeks. They had the house all to themselves. And it was raining. A fire would be lovely, and there was that soft afghan that was draped across one of the wing chairs in the library . . .

The kitchen was empty, too. A percolator stood in the centre of the table, filled with dark liquid, and two mugs stood beside it, but Quinn was nowhere to be seen. Paige frowned and turned back into the hallway. She peered into the empty sitting-room. Was he upstairs? Her pulse raced. Yes, he must be. He was probably in the guest bedroom, taking his clothes from the wardrobe, readying them for transfer back to his own room. To their room . . .

She was on the second stair when she heard a noise in the library. But she'd looked there. With a shrug of her shoulders, she padded along the hall and into the room.

No wonder she'd missed him the first time. He was far to the left of the door, almost hidden from view behind it. Paige stepped into the room, her bare feet making no sound on the carpeted floor. Quinn was standing in front of the campaign table, his back to her, and she watched as he lifted and twisted one of the brass corner gussets. A concealed drawer sprang open.

'Caught you red-handed,' she said with laugh. 'Secret drawers full of treasure, hmm?'

He spun around towards her. 'Didn't you ever hear of knocking before you enter a room?'

Her heart plummeted. 'I . . . I didn't know you . . . I didn't mean to intrude.' She stared at him in silence, and then she nodded. 'I'll be in . . . in my room.'

'Paige.'

'What?' She had to whisper the word to keep her voice from breaking.

He took an envelope from the drawer, put it in his jacket pocket, and slid the drawer shut with a click. When he looked at her again, there was a polite smile on his face.

'I'm sorry. I didn't mean to snap at you. You startled me, that's all.'

She nodded. 'That's . . . that's all right, Quinn. I . . .

I . . .' She looked down at her shoeless feet and then at him. 'I guess you didn't hear me. It's a habit of mine,' she said with a quick smile. 'Padding around barefoot . . .'

Her voice drifted away. Why hadn't it occurred to her that things might be strained between them this morning? It would take time to ease into their new relationship. But they had all the time in the world. Years stretched ahead of them, years filled with love and discovery.

'I made coffee,' he said. 'It's in the kitchen. I'm sure it's not as good as Norah's, but . . .'

'It smells wonderful,' she said quickly, watching him as he walked to his desk and pulled open a drawer. 'Why don't you pour yourself a cup and drink it while I make breakfast?'

He slammed the drawer shut and pulled out another. 'Breakfast?'

Paige nodded. 'Something special. How about some pancakes and bacon? Or waffles—I'm pretty good at waffles. My father always loved my waff . . .'

Dear God, what had made her say that? Quinn straightened up and stared at her.

'Your father,' he said softly. 'Yes, how is he? You haven't mentioned him in quite a while.'

'He . . . he's fine,' she said quietly. 'I had a letter from home just the other day. He says things are . . . are quiet at the office.'

'Let's hope he keeps things that way.'

The flatness of his voice turned her blood cold. For the first time, she realised that he was dressed for business. It was Saturday, but instead of his corduroys and turtleneck sweater he was wearing a suit. And his raincoat was draped over the back of a chair. A flight bag stood on the floor.

'Are you . . . are you going somewhere?'

He snapped the bag shut. 'Yes, I am. I've business in Edinburgh. Didn't I mention it?'

'No, no, you . . . you didn't say anything about . . .'

'I thought I had,' he said briskly. He tossed the coat over his arm and started towards the door. 'Well, no matter. You won't be alone long; Norah's due back this evening.'

Paige's heart tumbled as she hurried after him to the front door. 'But . . . but when will you be back, Quinn?'

He stopped at the door. 'In a few days,' he said finally.

'A few days,' she repeated in a whisper.

He nodded. 'I'll be back by the end of the week.' He looked as if he wanted to say something more, but, after a pause, he turned and put his hand on the doorknob. 'We can discuss things then.'

'Discuss things?' She swallowed hard. She heard herself repeating everything he said, as if she were a mynah bird. 'I don't understand.'

'Us. You, me.' His voice was expressionless. 'There's no sense in going on like this, Paige. I want things settled.'

He opened the door and a gust of rain-chilled wind blew in from the street.

'I thought . . . I thought we'd done that last night when you . . . when we . . .'

He swung around and faced her. His eyes were as flat as the sea before a storm.

'We slept together. Don't try to make more of it than that.'

She felt the blood drain from her face. A horn blared outside, and Quinn turned away.

'My taxi is here. I've got to go, Paige.' His voice was brusque. 'We'll talk when I get back.'

'Quinn . . .'

But he was moving away from her, hurrying down the walk to the taxi. She watched as he opened the door and climbed inside; she watched until the black Austin merged with the grey, rainy street and disappeared.

She hardly remembered closing the door behind her.

CHAPTER TEN

THE LIBRARY was cool. A fire burned on the hearth, but the chill breath of the grey day had seeped into the room. Huddled in one of the wing chairs, staring into the dancing flames as she sipped a cup of bitter coffee, Paige tried to make sense out of what Quinn had said.

I want things settled.

She thought what had happened between them last night had done that.

We slept together.

But what they'd shared had been more than sex. Quinn knew that—he had to know it. Everything they'd done together last night, the wildly sweet hours of touching and kissing and learning, had been special.

Hadn't it?

Don't try to make more of it than that.

Her hand trembled as she put the cup down. Was that what she'd done?

She rose from the chair and walked to the french doors. What did she know of lovemaking? she thought as she drew aside the curtains and looked out at the rainswept garden. She had only the most limited experience. Maybe . . . maybe it was always supposed to be the way it had been last night.

Paige let the curtains fall into place. Not even she could believe that. She was inexperienced, but she was no fool. There was good sex and there was bad sex, just as there were good lovers and bad ones. And Quinn—Quinn was a skilled lover, a virile, handsome man in the prime of life.

He knew how to please a woman. God, yes, he knew.

Don't make more of it . . .

She'd spent the night in his arms, but he'd never once said, I love you. He'd called her his sweet Juliet, he'd told of the pleasure she gave him, of how much he wanted her, but what did that mean when you compared it to the simple words he'd never uttered?

Paige sank into the chair and stared into the fire. Suppose she'd only been kidding herself? Suppose, under all the laughter and the easy camaraderie, Quinn had never stopped hating her? What a special torture there would be in using her heart as well as her body.

When you want a man, I'll be there.

She remembered the night he'd made that cruel promise. But they'd both said things designed to hurt that night.

Last night, he'd thought she wanted Jack Ward.

She sprang to her feet. 'No!'

Her whisper trembled in the silent room. That was insane. If that were it, he'd have taken her callously. But he'd been tender and caring; he'd spent hours kissing her and touching her until she'd trembled in his arms and begged for for release.

I'll make love to you until you beg me to stop. And then I'll be free of you.

She gasped for breath, as if all the air had been suddenly drawn from the room. What was the matter with her? Quinn cared for her. She knew he did. Not just because of the way he'd made love to her; that was part of it, yes, but there were other things. They'd been happy together the past weeks. They'd gone places and done things and laughed and talked . . .

But never about what had brought them together. When she'd tried, Quinn had cut her short, and she hadn't forced the issue. Why run the risk of spoiling things? she'd told herself, just as she'd told herself they didn't have to talk about the past because they'd left it behind.

But that wasn't true. You never really left the past; the best you could do was hope to understand it. Then you could build a future.

Paige let out her breath slowly. That's what Quinn had meant when he'd said they had things to settle. Her heart lifted. Of course! She understood—and he was right. Making love, even falling in love, couldn't change the awful reason for their marriage. They had to talk about Alan and her father. Then they'd be free to begin their life together at last.

She was Mrs Quinn Fowler. Paige Fowler. Her lips turned up in a smile. Funny, she'd never let herself think that way before, but that was who she was. That was who she wanted to be. She was Quinn's wife . . .

The peal of the doorbell startled her. Paige sighed and walked through the entrance hall to the front door. Norah was back early, she thought. The rain had probably done it. Norah's sister lived far across London, two bus rides with a transfer between them, and on a day like this the buses were always late and the queues long.

'Did you forget your key, Norah?' Paige smiled as she opened the door. 'I'm glad you're back; I was just going to make myself a cup of tea . . .' Her words tumbled to a halt as she saw the tall, fair-haired figure on the doorstep. 'Father?' she said in disbelief.

Andrew Gardiner's expression was bleak. 'Hello, Paige. May I come in?'

She stared at him, and then she nodded and stepped aside. 'Yes, yes, of course. I'm just . . .' She caught her breath as the door shut behind him. 'Is something wrong at home? Is Mother . . .'

'Your mother's fine.'

Paige closed her eyes with relief. 'Thank God. I thought . . .'

Her father took off his coat and handed it to her. 'I suppose you might say I'm here on business,' he said slowly, watching as she hung the coat on the rack beside the door.

'Business?'

Her father nodded. 'Yes. Could we sit down somewhere, Paige?' He smiled apologetically. 'And I could use a drink. Brandy, if you have it.'

'But what kind of business?' she asked, staring at him. 'Quinn never said . . .'

'Brandy first, please. I had to wait for ever for a taxi at the airport.'

She nodded. 'Of course. Come sit by the fire and I'll get you a drink.'

He followed her into the library, watching as she took a snifter and poured a generous brandy.

'Thanks,' he said when she handed it to him. 'Cheers —isn't that what they say here?' He tossed the drink off in one swallow and inhaled through his teeth. 'Maybe you'd better have one of those yourself,' he said with a strange laugh.

She stared at him for a moment and then she nodded. 'Maybe I had,' she said, and she splashed some brandy into a glass. 'Now, Father, why don't you tell me what this is all about?'

'This is a lovely house you have, my dear.' He looked around the room. 'That's a Watteau, isn't it?' he asked, gesturing at the painting above the fireplace. 'Expensive.'

A chill began to move along Paige's spine. 'Quinn's not here,' she said, watching him.

He turned towards her. 'That's just as well.'

The chill grew more pronounced. 'But you said you were here on business, Father.'

'Yes. But it has nothing to do with your husband. This need only concern you and me.'

She stared across the room. 'What are you talking about?'

His eyes met hers and then slid away. 'I wouldn't have come to you if I had a choice,' he muttered. 'You must understand that, Paige. But I . . . I had nowhere else to turn, and . . .'

'Does Mother know you're here?'

Andrew Gardiner's head rose sharply. 'Of course not. I . . . I just told her I had to go out of town on business.'

'For Mr Fowler?'

Her father laughed. 'Exactly.'

She took a deep breath. 'I think you'd better tell me why you're here.'

Her father nodded. 'Yes, all right.' He eyed the brandy bottle longingly. 'I don't suppose . . .'

'Father, please, what's this all about?'

'All right, Paige. I'll come to the point. I have to borrow some money from you.'

'Money? And you came to me?' She almost laughed. 'I have no money, Father.'

'Don't be ridiculous.' His voice was sharp. 'You married a fortune.'

'I married a man,' she said carefully. 'There's a difference.'

He shrugged. 'The point is, you have a lot of money, Paige. And I . . . I need some.'

She looked at him. 'For what?'

'What's the difference? I . . .'

Her chin rose. 'For what, Father?'

His eyes slid from hers. 'I . . . I borrowed some money.'

'But you promised Mother . . .'

Her father made an impatient gesture. 'No. I . . . I needed more than . . . I borrowed it from a different place.'

Paige's face paled. 'You mean, you embezzled from Fowler's again! Are you crazy? You swore . . .'

Andrew Gardiner waved his hand in dismissal. 'This

has nothing to do with Fowler's. It was a loan. From . . . from someone, a friend of a friend. If things had gone the way they should have, I could have paid it back easily. But . . .'

'But?'

He laughed uncomfortably. 'But things didn't.'

'What things?'

'It doesn't matter,' he said impatiently. 'What's the difference? Now I need . . .'

Paige lifted her chin. 'You need me to get you out of a scrape,' she said bitterly. 'The same as before. The only difference is that this time you've decided to tell me about it.'

Her father's mouth twisted. 'I don't know what that's supposed to mean, Paige.'

'Come on, Father, it's too late to play games. We both know why you were so eager to marry me off to Alan. I was to be the insurance that you wouldn't be prosecuted if you were caught.'

'It worked out,' he said defensively. 'You married well. And you have all this money.'

Paige stood up. 'My husband has all this money,' she said flatly.

'You have access to some of it, don't you?'

'I'm not going to get you out of this jam, Father. Tell whoever you've borrowed from that you can't . . .'

'Paige, listen to me. I know you—you don't think well of me. But I'm in real trouble this time. Think of your mother, if not me.'

'Tell him you'll pay him off bit by bit, that . . .'

'Christ almighty!' His voice rose in pain. 'They'll break my legs, don't you understand? I'll be found in some dark alley.'

'What are you talking about? You said you'd borrowed from a friend.' She stared into her father's eyes. 'A loan shark,' she said softly. 'That's who you owe, isn't it? A Shylock.'

'It was the only way I could get the money I needed.'

'But . . . they wouldn't really hurt you, would they? That kind of thing only happens in bad films.'

'It happens in real life, my innocent daughter. I . . . I've owed the money for some time. For several weeks. And if I don't pay by the day after tomorrow . . .' Andrew Gardiner's voice trembled. 'Just lend me what I need for a week. Two, at the most. I beg you, Paige.'

Paige sank down in the chair opposite him. 'A loan shark,' she whispered, her eyes on his. 'First you stole and now . . .'

'I didn't steal anything,' he said quickly. 'I borrowed. This is different.'

'Nothing's ever different,' she said sharply. Why had it taken her so long to see the truth? You couldn't just ignore things because they were unpleasant. Pushed into dark corners, shadows grew instead of dying.

'Paige.' His voice was low, heavy with desperation. 'Please . . .'

'Why?' she whispered. 'Why do you do it? I don't understand you.'

Gardiner leaped to his feet. 'Why do you think?' he cried. 'No risk, no gain. I always tried to tell that to you and your mother. But neither of you understood; you thought it was all a silly game.'

'We did understand. You wanted better things for us. But we had all we needed, Father. You gave us everything.'

He shrugged her words aside. 'Do you know what it's like to handle money for the rich when you have none of your own?' His eyes grew fierce. ' "Did we lose a few thousand today, Gardiner? Well, not to worry, there's more where that came from." ' The mimicry left his voice and he thrust his jaw forward. 'I'm as smart as any of them. Hell, the only difference between the people I've worked my life away for and me is how much risk they're willing to take.' He bent towards her. 'I could have made a fortune this time, Paige. I've got a formula for predicting the market that will . . .'

Her father was still talking, but Paige wasn't listening. How could she and her mother have been so blind? Perhaps it had simply been easier to smile at his get-rich schemes than admit the truth—that he had a dangerous obsession, an addiction that had finally driven him into a desperate corner.

In only Quinn were here. Quinn would know what to do. but he was gone; she didn't even have a number where she could reach him. And he wouldn't be back until the end of next week. And by then, her father might be . . .

'All right,' she said, 'all right. I'll lend you what you need.'

Her father laughed aloud. 'Bless you, child. I'll return every penny—with interest. My formula . . .'

'I don't want to hear about your formula,' Paige said sharply. 'You need help, Father. You . . .' A look at his face told her to save her breath. This wasn't the time for lectures. Besides, her father would no more see his problem than she or her mother had. With a sigh of resignation, she rose from her chair. 'Just let me get my cheque-book,' she said. 'How much do you need?'

He pursed his lips and ran his finger beneath his shirt collar. 'Ten thousand dollars.'

The words seemed to echo through the room. Paige stared at her father in silence for what seemed for ever.

'Ten thousand dollars?'

He nodded. 'I'll pay it back,' he said quickly.

'But I assumed—I thought you needed a few hundred.'

He laughed unpleasantly. 'I'd hardly have come this distance for a few hundred dollars, Paige. What I need is ten thousand.'

She shook her head. 'I haven't got it.'

'What do you mean, you haven't got it? Your husband's wealthy.'

'I have less than a thousand in my bank account, Father. In dollars, that's . . .'

'I know what it is,' he said angrily. 'That's impossible, Paige. You must have more than that.'

'It's all I have. The other accounts are in Quinn's name.' Paige looked at her father. 'I'm sorry,' she said softly. 'There's nothing I can do.'

Andrew Gardiner turned white. 'They'll kill me. They've done it before. The man who told me about these people— he warned me, he said he knew somebody who'd borrowed from them and couldn't repay and he . . . he just disappeared.'

Her heart thudded. 'Go to the police.'

'The police? That would only make things worse. You don't talk to the police about men like this, not if you want to stay healthy.' Her father sank into the chair again. 'You've got to think of something,' he said, running his hands through his fair hair. 'Surely you must have something of value.'

Her hand went to her breasts, protectively seeking Quinn's ruby before she remembered that it was on the table in the bedroom.

'Jewellery,' her father said, as if he could read her mind. 'He must have given you jewellery.'

'No,' she said quickly. 'Nothing.' *Not Quinn's ring. Never that.*

His eyes narrowed. 'It's my life we're talking about, Paige. You wouldn't hold out on me.'

'Father. I . . .'

'Think, girl,' he said roughly. 'Is there a safe in the house?'

'No,' she said again, and then, suddenly, she remembered coming into the library that morning and finding Quinn at the campaign table.

'Well?'

She nodded. 'There's a secret drawer . . .' She looked at her father. 'I don't even know if there's anything in it.'

'Open it,' he said.

Her eyes filled with anguish. 'It's wrong,' she whispered. 'I can't just . . .'

'What happens to me will be on your conscience for ever.'

She swallowed. 'All right,' she said softly. 'Wait in the hall.' She closed the library door after him and then walked slowly to Quinn's campaign table. Carefully, she lifted and twisted the brass corner gusset. It moved easily, and the concealed drawer sprang open.

There were several envelopes stacked neatly inside. The first held papers, the second Quinn's passport. Her heart skipped a beat when she came to the third.

The envelope contained money. American banknotes. She took them out and counted them. Eight, nine, ten thousand dollars.

Paige put the bills on the table and stared at them. How could she take this money? It was wrong. Until last night, she'd been Quinn's wife in name only. Whatever uneasy beginning they'd made might be wasted if she did this. She bowed her head. If only he were here.

But he wasn't. Her father had crossed an ocean to tell her his life was in danger. She riffled through the bills again. Would the money itself be important to Quinn? She doubted it. Her husband was wealthy—he'd spent as much money as she held in her hand right now the afternoon he'd taken her shopping.

What it came to was that she'd be taking the money without his knowledge or his permission. Stealing it. That was what she'd be doing—stealing it, and giving it to her father, a man Quinn had already once protected. But what choice did she have? She couldn't let her father be hurt. Certainly, Quinn would understand that.

She took a deep breath and opened the library door. 'Here,' she said, thrusting the banknotes at her father. 'Now, leave and never come to me for help again.'

Her father let out his breath. 'Thank you, dear child. Thank you. I swear, once I'm out of this, it'll never happen again.' He looked at his wristwatch. 'If I hurry, I can just make the next flight back. Would you phone for a taxi?'

The thought of having to make small talk while her father waited for a cab made her stomach knot. It seemed easier to bundle him into Quinn's Jaguar and drive him to the airport herself.

'I'll take you,' she said, snatching her coat from the rack. 'Quinn left his car. It's in the garage.'

Her father cleared his throat. 'Paige?' She paused, hand on the doorknob, and he ran his tongue over his lips. 'I know I haven't been the kind of father I might have been,' he said gruffly. 'But . . . but I love you, girl. I just wanted you to know that.'

He put his arms around her. The simple action stunned her. Had he ever hugged her before? If he had, she couldn't remember it. She stood still within his embrace and then, hesitantly, she put her arms around his neck.

'I . . . I love you too, Daddy,' she whispered.

A cold gust of air swept over them as the front door opened. Paige and her father sprang apart. The housekeeper stood in the open doorway, staring at them.

'Norah,' Paige said. 'I . . . I didn't expect you until this evening.'

The housekeeper lifted an eyebrow. 'So I see, ma'am. I thought I'd come back a bit early.' Her chin rose. 'I take it Mr Fowler's not here.'

'Quinn?' Paige felt a surge of colour in her cheeks. 'No,

no, he's . . . he's away. This is . . .' She turned to introduce her father, but then she thought better of it. There would be questions she didn't have time to answer. 'We were just on our way out.'

Norah sniffed. 'Indeed.'

Paige nodded. 'Yes. We're . . . we're in a rush, so if you'd just . . .'

The housekeepr stepped aside. 'What shall I tell Mr Fowler if he calls?'

'Tell him that . . .' Paige hesitated. 'Just tell him I've gone out,' she said finally.

Norah's mouth tightened. 'I understand, ma'am.'

'I don't know when I'll be back. Late, probably.'

The housekeeper sniffed again. 'Yes,' she said, 'yes, I can imagine.'

CHAPTER ELEVEN

PAIGE sighed wearily as she shut off the Jaguar's engine. She'd expected to get back late, but this was ridiculous. Hours had passed since she'd left for the airport. The afternoon had stretched into a cold, moonless night, and the rain, which had let up for a short while, had begun again.

The mews was silent, the house dark. Norah was probably asleep, Paige thought, and she felt a twinge of regret. Even the housekeeper, always polite although never really friendly, would have been a welcome companion tonight.

She let herself into the house and then leaned her back against the closed door. There was a throbbing pain in her temple. A tension headache, probably. It had been building ever since she'd left the house with her father hours before. Everything had conspired against her: traffic to Heathrow had been horrendous, and then there'd been an accident on the A4 that had resulted in a detour. And she still wasn't entirely comfortable driving on what she thought of as the wrong side of the road. By the time they'd finally reached the airport, her father had missed his flight.

'You don't have to wait around, Paige,' he'd said. 'I'll be fine.'

She'd nodded and started to leave, and then she'd sighed. 'Come on, Father,' she'd said, forcing a smile to her face. 'Let's get some coffee.'

Her father had switched from coffee to brandy after a while. 'I need something to relax me,' he'd said, and that was just what the brandy had done. He'd become nostalgic, even maudlin, explaining endlessly how he'd only wanted the best for her always, until finally Paige had told him that for a man who kept saying that, he certainly did some strange and unforgivable things. Still, when it was finally time to see him on board his plane, he'd hugged her and her eyes had misted.

'I'll repay every dollar,' he'd promised. 'You tell that to your husband for me.'

Paige sighed as she undid her coat. Before she could do that, she'd have to tell Quinn she'd taken all that money. God, she dreaded it! But he'd understand, if he listened with his heart, and she was sure he was ready to do that. When he came home, they'd put aside all the misunderstanding that separated them. Passion had brought them together, but only honesty and trust could make their marriage real.

The stairs looked as steep as a slope in the Rockies. And her head was beginning to pound. Well, she thought as she climbed slowly to the upper floor, some aspirin and a good night's sleep would fix it. A phone call from Quinn would be even more welcome. She wouldn't tell him about her father's visit over the phone—that was something best done face to face—but the sound of his voice would make her feel better.

She paused on the landing. Maybe he'd called while she was out. No, Norah would have left a message on the all table, and it had been bare. It was late, but not so late that he might not still call. She'd shower and put on her nightgown and hope.

The bedroom was dark. The curtains were drawn against the rainy night—Norah's work, she thought, sinking down on the edge of the bed. God, she was exhausted! Her father's visit had worn her out. Now there was a new set of problems added to the old.

She put her hand to her throat, searching, as always, for

the solace of Quinn's ring.

The ring! Where was it? Paige sprang to her feet, her heart thudding erratically while she fumbled for the ruby in its accustomed place between her breasts—and then she shut her eyes and blew a sigh of relief.

What was the matter with her? The ring was on the bedside-table, where she'd left it after breaking the chain when she and Quinn . . .

But it wasn't. The other table, then. She must have forgotten.

But the ring was gone. She'd lost it. She . . .

'Stop it,' she whispered aloud. 'Ruby rings don't just walk off. It must be somewhere. It . . .'

'It is.'

Light flooded the room. 'Quinn?' Paige stared into the corner in disbelief. 'Quinn,' she said again, and laughed. 'You scared the life out of me.'

He was leaning against the wall, still dressed as he had been that morning. A smile curved over his lips.

'Surprise, darling,' he said. 'I'm back early.'

There was something strange about his eyes, she thought. The colour seemed muted. Almost dulled.

'Aren't you glad to see me, Paige?'

She took a step towards him. 'Of course. I'm just surprised you're back so soon. A week, you said.'

'So I did.'

'Is . . . is everything all right? You sound strange.'

He nodded. 'Everything's fine. Why wouldn't it be?'

It wasn't. There was a dark undertone in his voice, a warning that chilled her. Could he know about her father and the money? No, of course not. It was just her guilty conscience playing tricks.

She smiled at him. 'You should have called. I'd have met you at the airport.'

His glance drifted over her. 'How would you have

managed that, Paige? You were out all evening.'

Her breath caught. 'How did you kn . . .' She looked down at herself, at the raincoat she'd forgotten to take off, and then back at him. 'Right. I was out—for a while.'

He smiled coolly. 'And you're going out again?'

'Going ou . . . oh, no, no, I just forgot to hang my coat away. I . . .'

'Of course, you were going out again.' His lips drew back in a parody of a smile. 'After you found this.'

She looked into his outstretched hand. The ruby ring, pulsing with light, blazed in his palm.

'My ring,' she said with relief. 'Thank goodness! I was afraid . . .'

'You were afraid you'd lost it. And that woud have been hell, wouldn't it? After all, it's quite valuable.'

It reminds me of the night we met, of how much my life has changed, of how much I love you.

That was what she wanted to say, but the look on his face stopped her. There was something wrong. She could see it in his eyes. They were as cold as she'd ever seen them.

Did he know about her father's visit? No, he couldn't. He . . . *Norah!* Norah had told him. Paige hadn't introduced them, but all the housekeeper had to do was describe the man she'd seen—tall, fair-haired, older—and Quinn would know who it was. Her breathing quickened. Had she closed the secret drawer in the campaign table? Maybe Norah had found it open. Maybe Quinn already knew everything.

'Quinn?' Her voice sounded breathy and high-pitched. 'How long . . . when did you get back?'

He smiled again, and she knew that she would remember the shark-like quality of his smile for as long as she lived.

'I thought you wanted your ring, Paige.' He held his hand out again. 'Go on, take it.'

She hesitated, and then her fingers closed around the ruby. For the first time, it felt cold, as if the flame in its heart had been quenched.

'Thank you,' she said. Her mouth tasted of ashes, and she swallowed hard.

His eyes fixed on hers. 'You'll want to get that chain fixed. Hell, you can't tell what bed you'll lose it in next time.'

Her head rose sharply. He was smiling, as if what he'd said had been meant as a jest, but every instinct told her otherwise. Something terrible was happening. Something unknown.

She took a step forward. 'Quinn. What is it? Why did you come back so soon?'

His mouth twisted. 'Not soon enough, Paige.'

Her pulse began to race. 'What . . . what do you mean?'

'Come on, sweetheart. Don't play dumb. You're a lot of things, baby, but not dumb. Unlucky, maybe—but never dumb.'

Her heart turned over. Slowly, she raised her eyes to his and looked into their blue-green depths.

'You know, don't you?'

His expression was grim. 'Yes, I know. I know all of it.'

'How . . . how did you find out?'

'Norah's been with me for years, Paige. Did you think she wouldn't tell me?' He clasped her shoulders in his hands. 'I telephoned this afternoon, when I realised I . . . when I realised I hadn't left a number where I could be reached in an emergency.' His voice twisted with darkness. 'She told me about your . . . your guest. I came home as soon as I hung up the phone.'

'And the money? Did I leave the drawer open?'

There was a hollow silence. 'No,' Quinn said, and he laughed bitterly. 'No, finding the cupboard bare was just an educated guess.'

Paige nodded wearily. 'I see.'

His breath hissed through his teeth. 'You see?' His hands

curled into the lapels of her coat, half lifting her from her feet. 'You see? Is that all you're going to say?'

She shook her head. 'No. I . . . I . . .'

Where to begin? she thought. Quinn was white-lipped with anger, and she knew she was guilty. It wasn't the best time to tell him anything, much less try and make him understand why she'd taken his money and given it to her father, but time was a luxury she no longer had.

'Well?' His voice was cold. 'Don't tell me you've run out of explanations, Paige. You never have before.'

'Quinn, please. I didn't want you to find out this way. I . . . I know you're angry . . .'

He laughed. 'Angry? Is that what you think I am?'

'Furious, then. But . . . but you don't know the whole story.'

His hold on her tightened. 'Don't waste your breath. I'm tired of your lies.'

'I've never lied to you,' she said quickly. 'I . . .'

'You've never done anything else.'

'That's not true. If you'd just listen . . .'

'What's the point in listening? I wouldn't believe you if you told me water was wet.'

'I was desperate. That's why I took the money. I . . .'

'Yes, I'll bet you were!' His voice grew bitter. 'You knew you wouldn't be able to get a penny out of me.'

Paige shook her head. 'No. I was sure if I explained things, you'd give me the money. But . . .'

'Come off it, Paige. I wasn't born yesterday.' His face darkened as he bent towards her. 'And why don't I hear you making up any sweet little stories about your visitor? Can't you think of a way to pretend your fair-haired gentleman caller was Saint Nicholas, come to pay an early visit?'

Her chin lifted. 'I'm not going to lie, Quinn. You know he was here. But he caught me by surprise. I had no idea . . .'

'You had no idea!' His voice mocked her cruelly as he drew her towards him. 'How long was he in my house?'

'Not long. I . . .'

'How long?' he demanded.

'I . . . I'm not sure. Twenty minutes. Half an hour . . .' Tears glistened in the corners of her eyes. 'I couldn't help it, Quinn. I . . .'

'Jesus, what kind of woman are you?' he roared as he flung her from him. 'Is that the only excuse you can offer? You couldn't stop yourself from . . . from deceiving me in my own home?'

'I know how it looks,' she whispered. 'But he begged me. I . . .'

She shrank back against the wall as he rushed towards her, his hand upraised and trembling with barely controlled rage. They stood facing each other for what seemed an eternity, until finally Quinn lowered his hand and turned away.

'Get out.'

No, she thought, no . . . 'Quinn,' she whispered, 'please listen to me.'

He spun towards her again and caught her by the wrist. 'Don't push me,' he said through his teeth. 'These past few hours, sitting in the dark, I've thought of a dozen different methods of vengeance. Listen to me, Paige. Leave while you still can.'

Tears began to spill down her cheeks. 'I beg you, just give me a chance to explain.'

She winced as the pressure of his fingers increased. 'You almost got away clean. Ten thousand dollars, the Jaguar—if you hadn't been so damned greedy . . .'

'What are you talking about? I . . .'

'How far had you gone before you realised you'd forgotten the ruby? Hell, the minute I saw it lying on the table, I knew you'd be back.' His fingers dug into the tender skin on the underside of her wrist. 'After all, there was no risk. I was supposed to be out of town.'

'Quinn, for God's sake—I came back because I live here. This is my home.'

'It was my own damned fault. I tipped my hand this morning, didn't I? I never said "divorce", but you know what I meant.' His voice dropped to a growl. 'And once you put that and our nuptial agreement together, you panicked. No money. No house. No car. Nothing.'

'No. No . . .'

His eyes burned with a dark fire as he pulled her closer. 'So you decided to take as much as you could. I guess it runs in the family.'

Paige shook her head wildly from side to side. 'What are you talking about? It wasn't like that. I . . .'

'But that's all right; it just adds to the list of wonderful things I'll tell Alan if you ever try to crawl back to him.' A smile as cold as the night lit his face. 'Starting with a graphic description of the things we did in bed last night.'

His words were a knife, twisting deep into her heart. 'You're lying,' she whispered. 'Last night meant something.'

'It sure as hell did, sweet Juliet. Remember when I said I'd never let Alan play with dangerous toys when he was little?' His mouth narrowed. 'Well, if I wanted to be sure he didn't pick up the toy again—if I wanted to be sure it couldn't hurt him any more . . .'

Tears spilled from her eyes. 'No,' she begged. 'Please.'

'Men are like boys, sweetheart. Somebody else's used toy has very little value to them.'

Her head fell forward. 'Why . . .' Her voice broke. 'Why did you wait so long to . . . to . . .'

'You've got a short memory, Paige,' he said, as the pressure of his hand became almost unbearable. 'I told you I'd make you beg me to take you. He pulled her to him, and his eyes blazed into hers. 'And you did.'

'No,' she said, but, even as she whispered the word, she knew he was telling her the truth. Only the foolishness of her own desperate heart had blinded her to it. This was real, not the night she'd spent in his arms. This was where the magic had taken her.

A sob caught in her throat. 'I'd give my life to take back what we did last night.'

His eyes darkened. 'Yes,' he whispered, 'I'll bet you would.'

He drew her against him before she could stop him, and his mouth swooped to hers in a hard kiss that made a mockery of the night they'd shared. Paige cried out, twisting against the roughness of his embrace, but it was useless. When he'd finished with her, he thrust her from him. They stared at each other, and then she wiped the back of her hand across her lips.

'You disgust me,' she said in a shaky whisper.

A muscle clenched in his jaw as he turned away from her. 'Get out of my house.'

Her hands trembled as she drew the edges of her raincoat together. 'You'll get your money back, Quinn. Every damned penny, if it takes me a lifetime.'

He laughed. 'Forget it. Hell, not every man gets to pay ten thousand bucks for a piece of . . .'

She fled the room before he could finish the sentence. Her high heels clattered down the steps and through the entrance hall. She had a sudden glimpse of Norah's face, frozen in righteous indignation, and then the door slammed shut behind her.

The streets of London were cold and dark, the fog thick as she'd ever seen it. Anger hurried her along the pavement, towards the faint lights glowing beyond the mews. Anger gave her a destination—the only hotel she knew—

Claridge's, not far from Quinn's house in Mayfair. Her steps faltered a bit when she entered the elegant lobby, looking bedraggled in her wet raincoat, with her hair plastered to her head. She had no luggage, and the desk clerk looked properly sceptical.

'Have you a reservation, madam?'

Paige swallowed. 'No.'

The clerk smiled politely. 'In that case, I'm afraid . . .'

Without thinking, Paige lifted her chin. 'I'm Mrs Quinn Fowler,' she said, and the words seemed a magic incantation.

She was led to a corner suite. A basket of fruit and a pot of tea appeared, her wet coat and wetter shoes disappeared, to be returned dry and clean the next morning.

The manager himself accompanied the chambermaid who brought her clothing to her.

'This was found in your coat pocket, Mrs Fowler.' His voice held reproach.

Paige knew what it was was even before he held the ruby ring out to her. The sight of it put the first crack into the wall of anger that surrounded her. Her heart gave a tremulous lurch; it took effort to keep from reaching out for the ring.

'Thank you,' she said. 'If you'd just leave it on that table—and I'd like my bill, please. I'm leaving this morning.'

She wrote a cheque for an amount that made her turn pale. But there was just enough in her account to provide for the night's lodging as well as the fare to New York from Heathrow. Yet when she stood in the queue at the British Airways ticket counter, she found herself backing away in confusion. Before she knew what she was doing, she was following the signs to the Tube that would take her back to London.

Staying in England made no sense. Returning to

Claridge's, a place she could ill afford in her circumstances, made no sense, either. At least, that was what she thought—until she was once again standing in the handsome lobby of the venerable hotel. Then, with a terrible rush, the truth came to her.

She hadn't come to Claridge's last night because of its proximity to the house, she'd come because of the memories it held. Quinn had brought her here days before, mysterious and close-mouthed, smiling with pleasure when she exclaimed with delight at the reason for their visit.

'High tea,' he'd said, watching her face. 'The way it used to be done and hardly ever is any more.'

'I feel like royalty,' she'd whispered with a grin after a liveried server had brought delicate sandwiches and pastries.

'That's how you look,' Quinn had said, his eyes hot on hers. 'Like a fairy-tale princess.'

It had been such a lovely moment—and she'd believed it, believed in what she'd seen in his face when he'd looked at her, what she'd heard in his voice. And there had been other moments, other days, all of them made up of memories her heart refused to relinquish. She could not bring herself to leave them.

It was why she couldn't leave London.

She cabled home, afraid that her mother might phone her at the house in Mayfair, afraid, too, of what she might give away in her voice if she placed a call to the States. She was not yet ready to talk about what had happened; she was even less ready to try and explain why she wasn't heading home. The cable bubbled with enthusiasm.

'Off to Africa on photographic safari,' it said. 'Will be deep in the bush for weeks. Will get in touch when possible. Love . . .'

By day's end, she had a roof over her head. It wasn't much, just a tiny garret bedsitter on a shabby street off

Earl's Court.

'There's a one-ring burner, luv, and you only have to share the bath with the gent down the hall.'

Paige took it without hesitation. The room was dark and it smelled of damp, but it was cheap and clean. The landlady looked at her suspiciously when she said she had no luggage, but then her jaundiced gaze swept over her new tenant, lingering on the dark shadows beneath Paige's eyes and the tremor in her lips, and she clucked her tongue.

'I'll bring you a nice cup of tea,' she said. 'You look as if you could use it.'

Days turned into weeks. The holidays approached; everyone always talked about the old-fashioned beauty of a Dickensian Christmas and, even in the midst of her despair, Paige caught glimpses of the joy and excitement that swept London. Those moments were the worst of all, because they seemed to give a special and terrible emphasis to the pain that engulfed her. She was grateful when the holiday season finally ended, but her gratitude faded under the onslaught of a sudden January freeze. One bitter night, her landlady appeared at the door.

'Thought you might like some extra blankets,' she said. 'And there's this old electric kettle, if you can use it.'

The last was just a bit of polite nonsense, and both women knew it. Paige had use for almost anything that came her way. Her rent was cheap, but there were other expenses. Food. Clothing. And, although she bought only the simplest and most inexpensive of both, her meagre supply of funds was fast dwindling. She'd emptied all her money from her bank account the day she'd first rented the garret room, as if by having the cash close at hand she could somehow make it grow. But, of course, she couldn't.

She was worried. She needed a job—that was obvious. But there were none—at least, none for which she was qualified. Her situation grew as grim as the weather, her despair as deep. And, all the time, there was a little voice whispering deep inside her.

What are you doing here? it asked.

At first, she had no answer. Memories had kept her here, but after a while the memories began to lose focus, like old photographs kept too long in a box.

Why not go home? the voice whispered one night, while she slept. Paige blinked her eyes open and sat up in the dark room, shivering with cold.

The answer came swiftly, carried on the moan of the wind and the lash of the rain.

She couldn't leave London. Quinn was here—and that meant she had to be here, too. She loved him still, despite what he'd done to her, and she would always love him. He had used her, debased her, hurt her more deeply than she'd dreamed possible, but nothing could change what she felt for him.

She tossed aside the blankets and stumbled across the room, unmindful of the sharp cold. Her shoulder-bag stood on a scuffed wooden table near the door. She picked it up and tumbled the contents out, searching among the tissues and coins and crumpled bills until her hand closed around her ruby ring. Her eyes shut as she remembered the terrible night in Quinn's house when the stone had seemed to grow cold. The tears she'd so long kept inside her finally streamed down her cheeks. When at last she slept, it was with the ring clutched tightly in her hand, as if her chilled fingers might be warmed by the flame that had once burned within it.

In the morning, Paige stood at a jewellery counter in Harrods, chin high, undeterred by the stares of those who had difficulty reconciling the young woman in the cheap coat and vinyl boots with the customer who politely insisted that yes, she did, indeed, want to buy that rather expensive gold chain. The cost of her purchase diminished her remaining funds considerably, but the heavy weight of the chain and the security of the clasp as she hung the ruby around her neck brought a smile to her lips.

This chain wouldn't break, she thought, touching her hand to the ring as it swung against her breasts. She vowed never to remove it again.

When she returned to the rooming-house, she knocked at her landlady's door. It was time to pay the rent. The gold chain swung forward, the ruby catching the light, as she rummaged in her purse.

'That's a handsome bauble,' her landlady said. 'I could get you a nice bit of money for that, luv.'

Paige's reply was swift and heated. 'Never,' she said, touching her hand to the stone. 'I'll never part with this.'

Was it her imagination, or did the ruby suddenly seem to pulse with heat again?

As January slipped into February and February edged into March, something new was added to her despair, a lethargy that seemed to grow with each day that passed, until finally it was so intense that she found it difficult to get out of bed in the mornings. She told herself it was time to stop behaving so foolishly. People didn't die of broken hearts, after all. Life didn't stop for lack of love.

But all her silent, middle-of-the-night talks with herself did no good. Her sense of exhaustion grew as did her depression. And there were other things: the sight of food nauseated her, which was all right, really, when she thought of how desperate she was to save her dwindling funds. But she felt a flash of concern when she noticed a faint tremor in her hands. What prospective employer would want to hire a typist whose hands shook? Her feet began to swell, especially after she'd spent hours marching the streets of London, trying to find work. Still, Paige would have ignored all of it—until that afternoon at thr temporary employment agency

The smartly dressed young woman at the front desk smiled at her as she pushed open the door.

'Hello,' she said. 'I'm glad to see you, Miss Gardiner.'

Paige looked at her in surprise. 'You remember me?'

The woman nodded. 'I thought of you just this morning. I have a new client—an American lady. She's going to be here for a month or so, and she wants a secretary. She says she'd like someone who'd been to the States, and I thought of you.' The woman's eyes narrowed. 'See here, Miss Gardiner, are you ill?'

Paige shook her head, although the motion sent a wave of nausea through her. 'No, no, I'm fine. Really. I . . .'

'Well, you don't look it,' the woman said briskly. 'Are you sure it's not the 'flu? Everyone's down with it.'

Paige managed a smile. 'I'd better not be ill. I can't afford it.'

The woman looked at her. 'If you're ill, the job's out, Miss Gardiner. I think you'd better stop at the clinic and have the doctors take a look at you.'

'It's not necessary, I assure you.'

'I can't send you on an interview with the 'flu.'

The clerk's voice was firm. Paige stared at her and then she sighed. When you balanced a job against half an hour spent being poked at by a doctor, the job was the clear winner.

'All right,' she said. 'I'll get a clean bill of health and be back.'

What if it was the 'flu? she thought as she stepped into the street. The doctor would prescribe aspirin and fluids and bed rest. It was bed rest she couldn't afford, she thought wryly. The job wouldn't wait that long.

But 'flu only took a week. And, at the end of it, she'd feel well again. Spring was coming; surely there would be other jobs. Her steps quickened. It would be a relief to find she had some simple thing that could be treated and cured. The 'flu would be an improvement over a broken heart.

Later, Paige would wonder at her incredible stupidity.

CHAPTER TWELVE

ST JAMES'S PARK was all but deserted in the chill of late afternoon. An occasional walker hurried by, shoulders hunched against the wind, and once Paige heard the distant bark of a dog. Other than that, she was alone.

How long had she been standing on the little bridge that crossed the dark water of the lake? One hour, two—perhaps an eternity. She didn't even remember coming here, but she had, unconsciously retracing part of the route she and Quinn had followed her first day in London, walking past the Houses of Parliament, past the Horse Guards, and into the park. But she'd seen none of what she'd passed. Her mind was in torment, posing questions that had no answers and offering answers that had no meaning.

A gust of wind blew across the lake, and Paige shivered beneath its cold caress. It was cold here, and damp. But there was no where else to go. She couldn't face her garret room and its aura of not-so-genteel poverty. And there was no sense in going back to the employment office. What could she say to the sympathetic clerk who'd found her a job?

I went to see a doctor and you can stop worrying; I haven't the 'flu.

Perhaps she could make a joke of it. She could say, *what I have isn't catching at all. I'm just a little bit pregnant.*

A little bit pregnant. It was like the punchline to a bad joke, except there wasn't anything funny about it. The doctor had examined her from head to toe, and then he'd called her into his office.

'You're about three months gone,' he'd said without preamble.

Paige had stared at him in disbelief. 'What?'

'You're pregnant. And it's a good thing you came in to see us when you did. Without proper care, you might have lost your baby.'

He'd gone on and on, telling her the things she had to do, and she'd listened, even though a stubborn part of her had kept thinking that surely all this had nothing to do with her. How could she be pregnant? There had only been that one night with Quinn . . .

. . . that one long night, when he'd turned what she felt for him against her.

She couldn't keep this baby. It would forever be a reminder of what Quinn had done to her . . .

. . . that one wonderful night, when he'd made love to her until the sky was streaked with tender rose and pale gold . . .

A night she would never forget. Quinn had taken her to his bed in anger, but then the magic that had brought them into each other's arms on a Connecticut beach had returned. Daylight had banished it, but that was the way magic was. It could only live with night hopes and moonlit dreams.

But the fruit of that night would be real. Their child would be a reminder of the magic that had almost been.

Paige had felt her heart fill with a fierce pride, and she'd heard herself assuring the doctor that she would do whatever had to be done to safeguard the child growing in her womb.

She needed nutritious food, he'd said. Lots of it. She was too thin. Had she been eating too many carbohydrates and not enough protein? And she mustn't exert herself. A couple of days in bed just now might be a good idea. She was to take long naps.

The list went on and on, and Paige kept nodding in

agreement. Reality hit only after she'd left the clinic. She stood on the pavement, shivering in her too-thin coat, and wondered how on earth she was going to manage. That was when she'd started walking, slowly, carefully, conscious of the life within her, until she'd found herself in the park, staring down at the dark water, her euphoria fast fading.

She shivered again and looked up. Someone was coming; she could hear the steady sound of approaching footsteps. It was a bobby, and even at a distance she could see that he was watching her. Paige sighed and lifted her elbows from the railing. It was time to move on, anyway. There was nothing to be accomplished standing here.

What she needed was money. That was what it came down to. Fruit, vegetables, milk, fish, eggs—all were far more expensive than the pasta she'd been living on. And she needed another coat: she'd bought a cheap one at an outdoor market at the start of winter, but it wasn't heavy enough to keep her warm.

The doctor had said no exertion. Was climbing the four flights of stairs to her garret room exertion? She hadn't thought to ask, but it seemed logical that it would be.

The street blurred suddenly, and Paige reached out to a nearby lamp-post and grasped it for support. She knew, almost to the last tenpence, how much money remained in her wallet. It was barely enough to pay the rent for another couple of weeks and buy some proper groceries. There was no way she could afford any of the things she needed if she were to keep her baby.

Quinn's baby.

Turning to him was, of course, out of the question. She knew no one else in London; she was alone. There was really no choice. She had to go home. There would be questions, but Paige knew her mother's heart well. Janet Gardiner would kiss her and welcome her, and she would stay at her side through the months ahead.

The Fowlers. How could she have forgotten them? What would happen when they learned she was pregnant? They would notify Quinn, and then the whole sordid story would come out. He would tell them why he'd thrown her out, he would tell them of her theft and her father's theft. He might even refuse to acknowledge the legitimacy of the child she carried. The scandal would be unbearable in a town like Greenwich.

Her hand went to her breast and she felt for the ring.

'You could always sell that for a lot of money, luv.'

She drew in a deep breath and walked quickly towards the Underground.

She chose Bond Street by name and reputation. Surely there were shops there that bought and sold fine jewellery? She bypassed the first few, intimidated by their quiet elegance. But finally, on a narrow side street, Paige squared her shoulders and pushed open the door of a small shop. She stood still, savouring the most welcome warmth.

'Yes, ma'am? May I help you?'

The proprietor was elderly. He shuffled towards her from the back room, smiling politely, even when he was close enough to see that she was hardly dressed the way she was sure most of his clients did.

Paige nodded. 'I hope so,' she said nervously. Her hands trembled as she unbuttoned her coat and the heavy sweater beneath, then reached to the nape of her neck. 'I . . . I want to sell something . . .'

The old man smiled politely. 'I'm afraid we don't buy jewellery, my dear.'

Paige's head rose. 'But your sign says . . .'

He nodded. 'We buy estate pieces. Heirlooms, antiques, things that have a special value . . .'

She heard the rasp of his breath as she unclasped the gold chain and drew the ruby ring from beneath her bodice.

'This has special value,' she said softly.

The old man's bushy white eyebrows rose. 'A family heirloom, hmm?'

Paige swallowed. 'Not . . . not really. It . . .'

The shop owner plucked the ring from her hand. 'Very handsome,' he said, but his eyes were on her face, not on the ruby. 'And very valuable.'

She nodded. 'Yes, I . . . it probably was. I . . .'

Her words fell into silence. The ruby lay in the old man's hand, the dark fire in its heart burning fiercely. She thought of the night Quinn had given it to her.

'When you look into the stone,' he'd said, 'think of me. Think of how it will be between us.'

She reached out quickly and took the ring from the shop owner's hand. 'The ring isn't for sale.'

His eyebrows rose even higher. 'But you said . . .'

'I want to sell the chain.' Paige's voice was steady. 'It's of very fine quality, as you can see.' She slipped the ring free and pushed the chain across the counter to him. 'Go on, take a look.'

'Where did you get that, young woman?'

'Harrods. But I'm sure they won't take it back. I don't have my receipt, or the box it came in, and . . .'

'Not the chain,' he said impatiently. 'The ring. Where did you get it?'

She swallowed. 'It . . . it was a gift,' she said. 'Look, if you're not interested in buying the chain . . .'

'Let me see the ruby.'

Reluctantly, she opened her hand and held the ring out to him. He took it and held it to the light. Then he took a loupe from his pocket and put it to his eye. At last, he pursed his lips and his flat gaze met hers.

'A gift, hmm?'

Paige nodded. 'Yes.'

'And you don't want to sell it.'

She shook her head. 'No. Just the chain. I . . .'

'All right,' he said, and he named a sum that was barely half what she'd paid.

'That's no good,' she said quickly, scooping up the chain. 'I need much more than that. I . . .'

The old man's eyes fixed on her. 'Yes, I'm sure you do,' he said, and she felt herself flush as he looked her over slowly.

'That's right, I do.' She stood her ground, knowing all too well how she looked. 'So, if that's your best offer . . .'

'Five thousand.'

She stared at him in stunned amazement. 'What?'

'I'll give you five thousand pounds for the ring.'

'I told you, it's not for sale. I . . .'

He shrugged. 'Ten.'

'Ten thousand pou . . .' She blinked. 'Are you joking?'

The old man smiled. 'All right. Twenty.'

Paige grasped the edge of the counter. 'You're crazy,' she whispered.

'Twenty-five, then. You'll just have to wait while I make a quick phone call . . .'

'You *are* crazy!'

'I have to call my bank. I don't keep that kind of money lying around.' He peered at her and then he sighed. 'Thirty thousand, and that's absolutely my final offer.'

She tore her eyes from his and stared at the ruby lying like a burning coal in her hand. Thirty thousand pounds. It was incredible. She had never seen that much money at one time in her life. If you added up what she'd earned during all the years she'd worked, you still wouldn't reach that much.

Conversions from pounds sterling to dollars and back again flashed through her head. Dear heaven, how far such an amount would go! She could rest, eat properly, have her baby, take her time about finding the right job after the child was old enough to leave with a sitter . . .

'No.' The word burst from her, and she closed her hand around the stone.

The old man's eyebrows rose. 'No?'

Paige shook her head. 'No,' she whispered. 'I . . . I could never sell my ring. It . . . it . . .'

'Look, you need the money. Let me make a call, and then . . .'

'You don't understand.' Her voice rose. 'This ring . . . this ring means more to me than all the money in the world. I . . . I'll think of something. I'll . . . I'll . . .'

The shop spun away. She saw the old man's look of surprise, heard herself make a sound that was part moan, part cry, and then she was falling, falling, spinning in a circle of bright light towards a narrowing cone of darkness, and as she fell into it, she heard the old man's voice telling her she'd be all right, she'd be fine, she'd be . . .

The darkness swallowed her.

Images. Dreams. Faces, shifting in and out. Men in white jackets. A siren, and a swaying ride through darkening streets. Voices and more faces, all taut with concern. Bright light, the prick of a needle, the softness of sheets and blankets, and then a voice, a persistent voice, pleading with her, urging her, trying to lure her from the darkness that still held her. A voice she knew.

'Paige.'

She tried to answer. But she was so weary. So weary . . .

'Paige, my love . . .'

She stirred restlessly.

'Paige—open your eyes. Look at me, Paige. Look at me.'

She wanted to. She wanted to lift her eyelids and see who was speaking to her in that hoarse, intense whisper, see who was holding her hand, but there was a comfort in the darkness. It would be so much simpler to stay within its embrace . . .

Lips brushed softly over hers. 'Please, darling. Look

at me.'

Darling. That was what Quinn had called her, but never as if he meant it. He'd never said it this way . . .

'Paige. Sweet Juliet. My love.'

Her heart leaped. She knew the voice, the touch, the feel of the lips against hers.

'Quinn?' Her whisper was hesitant, breathless. It took all the strength she possessed to say his name.

His hand caught hers, and she felt the warmth of his breath against her face.

'Paige. Thank God.'

'Quinn,' she sighed, and slowly her lashes lifted from her cheeks.

Her heart filled with happiness. It was Quinn. He was bent over her, his face only inches away, and when she looked into his eyes she knew that she could live on what she saw there for the rest of her life.

He cupped her face gently in his hands and brushed his lips against hers. If this was a dream, she hoped never to awaken. She whispered his name again, savouring the taste of it on her tongue.

'Don't talk,' he said fiercely. 'Not until I'm sure you're all right.'

She looked past him, seeing for the first time the white walls, the institutional ceiling lights, the impersonal furnishings of a hospital room.

'What happened to me? Where . . . ?' She struggled upward as he let go of her and stepped back from the bed. 'Don't leave me.' Panic threaded her voice. 'Quinn . . .'

'We just want to take a look at you, Mrs Fowler.' The voice was soft, filled with tones of professional reassurance. It belonged to a woman—a nurse, Paige realised—who smiled as she drew the curtains around the bed. 'This will only take a minute. Your husband will be just outside.'

Your husband. The phrase was like a lifeline. Paige caught it to her, clung to it while a white-coated physician bent over her.

'My baby,' she whispered, and her heart lurched in fear.

'Your baby's fine,' he said finally. She heard the door open, and then the curtains were drawn back. 'You're a very lucky young woman.'

'And very foolish.' It was Quinn's voice, stern and cold. 'Thank you, Doctor,' he said, and then they were alone.

Paige watched him as he walked towards her. His eyes were dark, his mouth narrow. Anger was etched into his face. Her pulse began to race. What a fool she was! Of course, she'd been dreaming. Quinn was here—that was real enough. But one look told her that he couldn't have whispered tender endearments to her only moments ago or kissed her as if she were precious to him.

She knew what had happened. She had fainted, and the shop owner had called for a ambulance. The hospital authorities had gone through her bag, found Quinn's name on the cheque-book she no longer used, and called him. As for the rest, none of it had happened. His kisses, his soft words, were things her heart wanted so badly that she'd imagined them. It was like the time she was a little girl and she'd had her appendix out. She'd come out of the anaesthesia slowly, certain her fairy godmother was talking to her. But it had been her mother, urging her to open her eyes and . . .

Paige turned her face away. She didn't want to see the darkness in Quinn's eyes. It was better to remember the dreams that had been hers as she regained consciousness.

He stopped beside the bed and stared down at her. 'Look at me,' he demanded.

She turned to him slowly. 'I . . . I'm sorry they bothered you,' she said. 'I guess I should have disposed of anything with your name on it, but . . .'

He put his hands on his hips. 'Have you been in London

all these weeks?'

Paige nodded. 'Yes.'

'Here,' he said, 'in the same damned city as me.'

She nodded again. 'I didn't ask them to contact you.'

'Why in hell didn't you go back to the States?'

'I . . .' She swallowed. 'I just didn't.'

One dark eyebrow rose. 'I asked you a question.'

Because I couldn't leave you. 'I don't know,' she whispered.

'You don't know.' His voice was flat.

Paige closed her eyes. 'Does it really matter? I . . . I've decided to go home now. I . . .'

She heard the hiss of his breath. 'You're damned right you're going home. Now. Just as soon as you're dressed.'

He was so angry! Tears slipped from beneath her lashes and she wiped her hand across her eyes.

'I . . . I don't have the money for a plane ticket, Quinn. I can't afford . . .'

'Come on.' Her eyes opened as she felt his arm slide around her shoulders.

'What are you doing?' she asked, even though the answer was obvious. He was sitting her up, drawing back the covers, fumbling at the tie of the ill-fitting hospital gown draped over her. 'Quinn . . .'

She put her hands to the neck of the gown, but he pushed them away. 'What does it look like?' His voice was rough. 'I'm helping you dress.'

Paige shook her head. 'No,' she whispered as he slid the gown off her shoulders. 'Quinn, don't. I don't need any help. I . . .'

The gown fell to her waist. 'Yes, you do, damn you,' he growled. 'Now, stop arguing and . . .'

She looked up as his words died away. His eyes swept across her, to her throat, to her breasts, and then his gaze returned to her face.

'Paige,' he whispered. His hand touched the curve of her breast and she closed her eyes.

'Don't,' she said sharply.

'Paige,' he said again, 'listen to me.'

She shook her head and pushed his hand from her. 'No,' she said. What was he trying to do? Was he trying to prove his mastery of her body? But they both knew about that; it was what had brought them down this dark pathway in the first place. 'The nurse can help me. Not you.'

Blood darkened his face. 'I'm still your husband,' he gowled. 'Now, lift your arms.'

'Quinn, please . . .'

His eyes blazed into hers. 'Do as I say, Paige.'

She closed her eyes as he eased something silky over her head. He drew it down her body and his hands brushed over her skin.

'Quinn, I beg you . . .'

The words caught in her throat. The last time she'd said that to him, the plea had come back to haunt her with a pain she would never be able to erase. She would never beg him for anything again, she told herself, and she sat still while he stripped away the gown and dressed her, not in the inexpensive clothing she'd worn, but in the soft silks and cashmeres he'd bought her the day after their wedding. His hands trembled as they touched her. She trembled, too; it was impossible not to feel the heat of his fingers on her flesh. His eyes caught hers, and she flushed and looked away.

'Does it hurt that much to feel my hands on you, Juliet?'

She stared at him. 'Does it . . . does it hurt?'

Quinn clasped her shoulders. 'Yes. When I touch you . . . Do you hate me so much?'

A sob rose in her throat. 'Hate you?' Paige caught her bottom lip between her teeth. 'Oh, Quinn . . .'

No. No more. Don't say anything, don't tell him anything,

don't add to the anguish and the humiliation you'll have to live with for the rest of your life . . .

His hands pressed into her. 'Sweet, sweet Juliet,' he murmured. 'My Juliet . . .'

'Don't!' It was a cry torn from her heart, and all the pain of the past months was caught within it. 'Don't,' she said again, and the whisper hung between them. 'Please, Quinn, if . . . if you ever thought anything good of me, if there was so much as a moment between us that mattered to you, let go of me.'

'Paige . . .'

She shook her head wildly. 'Just . . . just get out of here and leave me alone. I wish they hadn't sent for you. I . . .'

'Max called me.'

She raised her tear-swollen eyes to his. 'Max?'

Quinn nodded. 'The jeweller.' A quick smile came and went on his mouth. 'Sweet Juliet,' he said, stroking the hair back from her temples. 'Of all the jewellers in London, you went to the one who was bound to recognise that ring.'

Paige shook her head. 'I don't understand.'

'Max is the man who sold it to me.' He laughed softly at the look of surprise that flashed across her face. 'I bought it from him on impulse a couple of years ago. I was walking past his shop and I saw it in the window. It was the strangest damned thing—I don't like wearing jewellery, yet I knew I had to have that ring. There was something in the ruby's heart that drew me, a fire that burned with a heat like none I'd ever felt before—until I met you.'

His hands cupped her face and he looked into her eyes. His voice was so soft, it was a caress. What was he trying to do? Paige knew what he thought of her. He'd told her, often enough.

'Stop it,' she said. 'You have no right . . .'

'Max says you refused to sell him the ring. Why?'

'Quinn, please—why are you doing this? Why . . .'

He touched his lips to her temple. 'Why wouldn't you sell it to him, Paige?'

Pride darkened her eyes. 'He didn't offer enough,' she said. 'I knew the ring was worth more.'

His eyes fixed on hers. 'Max says you told him the ring meant more to you than all the money in the world.'

Tears trembled on her lashes. 'Please stop,' she whispered. 'Please . . .'

His mouth dropped to hers and he kissed her again. 'Tell me the truth, Paige. Why didn't you sell it?'

'Because it was all I had left of you.' She waited for the sound of his laughter, and when it didn't come, she inhaled shakily. 'All right, you've had your fun. Now let go of me.'

He put his hand on her abdomen. 'It wasn't all you had,' he said softly. 'You have our child growing beneath your heart.'

Her pulse raced. He knew. *He knew.* She waited for him to say something more, to warp his words with cruelty, but he was silent. Finally, she nodded.

'Yes,' she whispered.

Quinn frowned. 'But you weren't going to tell me about it.'

Her chin lifted. 'No.'

His brows drew together. 'I see. You were going to go on living God knows where . . .'

'I have a perfectly nice room off Earl's Court.'

'Yes,' he said, 'I can imagine. It probably goes with the way you look.'

Paige's eyes darkened. 'There's nothing wrong with the way I look.'

'The hell there isn't! You're too pale. Too thin. Too . . .' His arms tightened around her. 'Too beautiful,' he said, and he bent his head and kissed her.

She tried to pull away from him, but his arms held her fast. His mouth was hard and insistent, demanding response from hers. And then his kiss became gentler, filled with tenderness, until finally he was kissing her as he had the night they met, as he'd kissed her the night he'd made love to her. Everything she'd ever prayed he would tell her seemed to be contained in the kiss. She moaned softly as he gathered her closer to him, and her lips parted beneath his. If only he loved her. If only he cared.

But he didn't. He hated her. He thought she'd trapped his brother into marriage for the Fowler money and to protect her father. He thought she was a thief and a schemer and a tramp . . .

It took all the strength she had to twist free of him. 'Damn you,' she whispered. 'Damn you to hell, Quinn Fowler!'

'That's where I've been since you left me.'

She turned her head away so he wouldn't see the pain in her eyes. 'Do you hate me so much? You've already humiliated me enough. You . . .'

'I love you.' Her heart tumbled against her ribs as he whispered the simple words she'd waited so long to hear. 'I love you,' he said again. 'Do you hear me, Paige?' His hands clasped her shoulders and he looked into her eyes. 'I've always loved you, even when I tried to deny it to myself.'

Tears glistened on her lashes. 'Don't play with me, Quinn,' she whispered. 'I . . . I couldn't stand it. I . . . I love you too much.'

'Oh, Juliet!' His arms closed around her and he pressed her to his heart. 'I fell in love with you the first minute I saw you, in a ballroom full of hobgoblins. It didn't matter that I didn't know your name or anything about you. My heart told me all I needed to know.' He drew in his breath and let it out slowly. 'And then I learned who you were.'

'That I was Alan's fiancée,' she said unhappily. 'Quinn, I tried to explain. Alan knew I didn't love him. I let him talk me into our engagement. He said . . . he said we'd be happy, and I wanted to believe him. I never knew about my father and the money . . . He's sick,' she said in a rush. 'He's obsessed with winning . . .'

He pressed his lips to the top of her head. 'Hush, sweetheart. I know everything. I spoke with Alan. And with your father.' His arms tightened around her. 'He made a clean breast of things to your mother, Paige. She's convinced him to join a therapy group. They're sure they can help him.'

Paige shook her head. 'I don't understand. When did you talk to them?'

He sighed. 'The day after you left me. I flew to the States looking for you.'

'You did?'

Quinn nodded. 'Yes, darling. I found out I'd made a terrible mistake. You see, the day I went to Edinburgh, I phoned home to talk to you. Norah answered; she told me . . .'

'She told you my father had been to see me.'

Quinn shook his head. 'She told she'd found you in the arms of a tall, fair-haired man. I . . . I thought it was Jack Ward.'

Everything began to fall into place. 'You mean, you thought that terrible man and I . . . ? Oh, God!'

His laughter was bitter. 'Exactly. I put two and two together and came up with five. I think my conscience was almost grateful for the chance.'

Paige leaned back against his encircling arms and looked into his eyes. 'I don't understand,' she said softly.

There was pain in Quinn's smile. 'I was filled with guilt,' he said. 'You were right when you said I wanted you for myself. It was one thing to take you from my brother to protect him, but it was quite another to admit to myself that I'd fallen in love with you. I couldn't face the truth, Paige.'

He kissed the tip of her nose. 'That was why I didn't want to talk about the way I'd forced you to marry me.'

'Oh, Quinn, we should have trusted our feelings. I . . . I never came alive until I met you . . .'

His arms tightened around her. 'I'd never known a night like the one we shared, Juliet,' he whispered. 'When I woke up with you in my arms, I knew I had to get away and sort out my feelings. I didn't know what to believe. Were you the woman I'd learned to love, or were you the woman I'd accused you of being? Could I live with the knowledge that I'd have taken you from my brother, no matter what the circumstances?' He laughed softly. 'I wasn't gone half a day when I knew that none of the questions mattered. I loved you now, no matter what had happened in the past. It was our future that counted. I phoned home to tell you that.'

Paige closed her eyes. 'And Norah told you I'd been with a man. But . . . how did you learn the truth?'

He shrugged. 'I went looking for Ward. I wanted to kill him—but it turned out he and his wife had left the city early that morning. I realised he couldn't have been the man who'd come to the house.' He sighed. 'I began to search for you; I traced you to Claridge's and then to the airport—and your trail vanished. But I thought surely you'd flown back to the States—so I did, too.'

'Looking for me,' Paige said softly.

'Yes. That's when your father told me everything, and Alan flew home for the weekend.' He laughed. 'Would you believe he's courting a dark-eyed *senorita*?'

Paige smiled. 'I'm happy for him.'

Quinn nodded. 'Yes, but all I could think of was you.' He touched his lips to her throat. 'I've been going insane, darling, loving you, wanting you, worrying about what might have happened to you . . .'

Paige put her arms around his neck. 'I never left London,' she said. 'I loved you too much to put an ocean between us.'

'Juliet,' he murmured, 'sweet, beautiful Juliet.' She lifted her face to his. Quinn's kiss left her breathless, and then he put her from him gently. 'Are you sure that's all right for the baby?'

Paige smiled. 'I don't think love can ever hurt a baby.'

There was a discreet knock and the door swung open. 'Doctor says Mrs Fowler can leave any time now,' the nurse said pleasantly. 'He says if you need anything . . .'

Quinn smiled at Paige as he gathered her into his arms and rose to his feet. 'Do we need anything, my love?'

Paige pressed her lips to his throat. 'We need to go home,' she whispered.

His arms tightened around her. 'You are home,' he said, and she knew he was right.

Coming Next Month

1223 DEEP HARBOUR Sally Cook
Lucy had enjoyed the summer with her aunt's family in Minorca until strange things started to happen. Unafraid, she decides to investigate, only to discover that everything seems to lead back to a mysterious man in one of the villas....

1224 ONE HOUR OF MAGIC Melinda Cross
Robert Chesterfield had been full of light and laughter, while Daniel, his brother, had been so dark and brooding. Now, with Robert dead and Daniel providing her with a home and a job, Holly wonders how she can live with someone who hated the man she loved.

1225 LOVEKNOT Catherine George
Sophie's life had always been planned by those around her, particularly her father and brothers. Now everything is changing, and Sophie plans to change, too. Then why is it so difficult to leave her aloof, unapproachable boss, nicknamed Alexander the Great?

1226 REMEMBER TOMORROW Pamela Hatton
Powerful, arrogant Ross Tyler is fighting painful injuries as well as the belief that Cassie had deserted him after the car crash. When they finally chance to meet, Ross discovers that Cassie didn't even know he was alive.

1227 THE LOVING GIFT Carole Mortimer
David Kendrick falls in love with Jade at first sight—but that doesn't mean she has to put up with his impulsive pursuit. He might be charming, but since she's still running away from a hurtful past, surely it's better not to start anything?

1228 DON'T ASK WHY Annabel Murray
Why is the stranger in the astrakhan coat following her husband? Determined to find out, Giana's search soon leads her to greater confusion and a life of lies and subterfuge in the employ of the semireclusive Breid Winterton.

1229 MAN WITHOUT A PAST Valerie Parv
"Don't love me, Gaelle," Dan warns her, "for your own sake." But it is already far too late to tell her that. And neither of them can foresee just how impossible their love is....

1230 UNWILLING HEART Emma Richmond
O'Malley coped with being buried alive in an earthquake in Turkey—and having to dig her way out. But being kidnapped by a mysterious Frenchman, whom she knows only as Paget, is another matter entirely!

Available in December wherever paperback books are sold, or through Harlequin Reader Service:

In the U.S.
901 Fuhrmann Blvd.
P.O. Box 1397
Buffalo, N.Y. 14240-1397

In Canada
P.O. Box 603
Fort Erie, Ontario
L2A 5X3

Especially for you, Christmas from
HARLEQUIN HISTORICALS

An enchanting collection of three Christmas
stories by some of your favorite authors captures
the spirit of the season in the 1800s

TUMBLEWEED CHRISTMAS by Kristin James

A "Bah, humbug" Texas rancher meets his match in his
new housekeeper, a woman determined to bring the spirit
of a Tumbleweed Christmas into his life—and love into
his heart.

A CINDERELLA CHRISTMAS by Lucy Elliot

The perfect granddaughter, sister and aunt, Mary Hillyer
seemed destined for spinsterhood until Jack Gates arrived
to discover a woman with dreams and passions that were
meant to be shared during a Cinderella Christmas.

HOME FOR CHRISTMAS
by Heather Graham Pozzessere

The magic of the season brings peace Home For
Christmas when a Yankee captain and a Southern heiress
fall in love during the Civil War.

Look for HARLEQUIN HISTORICALS CHRISTMAS
STORIES wherever Harlequin books are sold.

Have You Ever Wondered If You Could Write A Harlequin Novel?

Here's great news—Harlequin is offering a series of cassette tapes to help you do just that. Written by Harlequin editors, these tapes give practical advice on how to make your characters—and your story— come alive. There's a tape for each contemporary romance series Harlequin publishes.

Mail order only

All sales final

HARLEQUIN'S "BIG WIN"
SWEEPSTAKES RULES & REGULATIONS
NO PURCHASE NECESSARY TO ENTER OR RECEIVE A PRIZE

1. To enter and join the Harlequin Reader Service, scratch off the pink metallic strips on all your BIG WIN tickets #1-#6. This will reveal the values for each sweepstakes entry number, the number of free books you will receive and your free bonus gift as part of our Reader Service. If you do not wish to take advantage of our introduction to the Harlequin Reader Service but wish to enter the Sweepstakes only, scratch off the pink metallic strips on your BIG WIN tickets #1-#4 only. To enter, return your entire sheet of tickets intact. Incomplete and/or inaccurate entries are not eligible for that section or section(s) of prizes. Not responsible for mutilated or unreadable entries or inadvertent printing errors. Mechanically reproduced entries are null and void.

2. Either way your unique Sweepstakes numbers will be compared against the list of winning numbers generated at random by the computer. In the event that all prizes are not claimed, random drawings will be held from all entries received from all presentations to award all unclaimed prizes. All cash prizes are payable in U.S. funds. This is in addition to any free, surprise or mystery gifts that might be offered. The following prizes are awarded in this sweepstakes: *Grand Prize (1) $1,000,000; First Prize (1) $35,000; Second Prize (1) $10,000; Third Prize (3) $5,000; Fourth Prize (10) $1,000; Fifth Prize (25) $500; Sixth Prize (5000)$5.

   *This Sweepstakes contains a Grand Prize offering of a $1,000,000 annuity. Winner may elect to receive $25,000 a year for 40 years without interest totalling $1,000,000 or $350,000 in one cash payment. Entrants may cancel Reader Service at any time without cost or obligation to buy (see details in center insert card).

3. Extra Bonus Prize: This presentation offers two extra bonus prizes valued at $30,000 each to be awarded in a random drawing from all entries received.

4. Versions of this Sweepstakes with different graphics will be offered in other mailings or at retail outlets by Torstar Corp. and its affiliates. This promotion is being conducted under the supervision of Marden-Kane, Inc., an independent judging organization. By entering this Sweepstakes, each entrant accepts and agrees to be bound by these rules and the decisions of the judges, which shall be final and binding. Odds of winning in the random drawing are dependent upon the total number of entries received. Taxes, if any, are the sole responsibility of the winners. Prizes are non-transferable. All entries must be received by March 31, 1990. The drawing will take place on or about April 30, 1990 at the offices of Marden-Kane, Inc., Lake Success, NY.

5. This offer is open to residents of the U.S., the United Kingdom and Canada, 18 years or older except employees of Torstar Corp., its affiliates, subsidiaries, Marden-Kane, Inc. and all other agencies and persons connected with conducting this Sweepstakes. All Federal, State and local laws apply. Void wherever prohibited or restricted by law.

6. Winners will be notified by mail and may be required to execute an affidavit of eligibility and release that must be returned within 14 days after notification. Canadian winners will be required to answer a skill-testing question. Winners consent to the use of their name, photograph and/or likeness for advertising and publicity in conjunction with this and similar promotions without additional compensation.

7. For a list of our most current major prize winners, send a stamped, self-addressed envelope to: WINNERS LIST c/o MARDEN-KANE, INC., P.O. BOX 701, SAYREVILLE, NJ 08871.

If Sweepstakes entry form is missing, please print your name and address on a 3" × 5" piece of plain paper and send to:

In the U.S.	In Canada
Harlequin's "BIG WIN" Sweepstakes	Harlequin's "BIG WIN" Sweepstakes
901 Fuhrmann Blvd.	P.O. Box 609
Box 1867	Fort Erie, Ontario
Buffalo, NY 14269-1867	L2A 5X3

© 1989 Harlequin Enterprises Limited   Printed in the U.S.A.

LTY-H119

Wonderful, luxurious gifts can be yours with proofs-of-purchase from any specially marked "Indulge A Little" Harlequin or Silhouette book with the Offer Certificate properly completed, plus a check or money order (do not send cash) to cover postage and handling payable to Harlequin/Silhouette "Indulge A Little, Give A Lot" Offer. We will send you the specified gift.

Mail-in-Offer

Item	A. Collector's Doll	B. Soaps in a Basket	C. Potpourri Sachet	D. Scented Hangers
# of Proofs-of -Purchase	18	12	6	4
Postage & Handling	$3.25	$2.75	$2.25	$2.00
Check One				

Name _____

Address _____ Apt. # _____

City _____ State _____ Zip _____

Indulge A LITTLE GIVE A LOT

ONE PROOF OF PURCHASE

To collect your free gift by mail you must include the necessary number of proofs-of-purchase plus postage and handling with offer certificate.

HP-2

Harlequin®/Silhouette®

Mail this certificate, designated number of proofs-of-purchase and check or money order for postage and handling to:

INDULGE A LITTLE
P.O. Box 9055
Buffalo, N.Y. 14269-9055